THE LAPTEV

VIRUS

Also by this author:

The Cantabria American School series:
BUENO (Book 1)
SINCO (Book 2)
BRUJAS (Book 3)

GRAMMY AND THE WILEY RACCOON

THE LAPTEV VIRUS

A Novel

by
CHRISTY ESMAHAN

Book cover artwork was done by Christy Esmahan and she holds the copyright thereto. The front cover image is a computer enhanced electron microscope photograph of a Pithovirus, a true giant virus discovered in Siberia. It was generously provided to me for use on the cover of this novel by Dr. Chantal Abergel & Dr. Jean-Michel Claverie, IGS, CNRS-AMU, France. The back cover is a photograph of an oil rig in the Laptev Sea area which is used with permission kindly granted by Graham Blackbourn, Director of Blackbourn Geoconsulting.

ISBN: 1507581955
ISBN-13: 978-1507581957
Library of Congress Control Number: 2015902502
CreateSpace Independent Publishing Platform, North Charleston, SC

Available from Amazon.com and other retail outlets.
Also available on Kindle

For Dr. John R. Stevenson,
and in memory of
Dr. Donald C. Cox,
Dr. Robert J. Brady and
Dr. Jnanendra K. Bhattacharjee,
truly outstanding Microbiology professors
and mentors
whom I hold fondly in my heart

"Strange things are slumbering in the permafrost—and some of them are able to wake up"

--Veronique Greenwood

ARCTIC MAP

Map is courtesy of Hugo Ahlenius UNEP/GRID-Arendal with modifications by Christy Esmahan
This map is used under the Share-Alike 3.0 Attribution. Unported Creative Commons License

PROLOGUE

On March 3, 2014, Geoffrey Mohan from the Los Angeles Times reported:

> A 30,000-year-old giant virus has been revived from the frozen Siberian tundra, sparking concern that increased mining and oil drilling in rapidly warming northern latitudes could disturb dormant microbial life that could one day prove harmful to man.
>
> The latest find, described online Monday in the *Proceedings of the National Academy of Sciences*, appears to belong to a new family of [giant viruses] that infect only amoeba. But its revival in a laboratory stands as "a proof of principle that we could eventually resurrect active infectious viruses from different periods," said the study's lead author, microbiologist Professor Jean-Michel Claverie of Aix-Marseille University in France.
>
> "We know that those non-dangerous viruses are alive there, which is probably telling us that the

dangerous kind that may infect humans and animals - that we think were eradicated from the surface of earth - are actually still present and [could be] eventually viable, in the [frozen] ground," Claverie said.

With global warming making northern reaches more accessible, the chance of disturbing dormant human pathogens is increased, the researchers concluded.

Average surface temperatures in the area that contained the virus have increased more steeply than in more temperate latitudes, the researchers noted.

"People will go there; they will settle there, and they will start mining and drilling," Claverie said. "Human activities are going to perturb layers that have been dormant for 3 million years and may contain viruses."

[...] Claverie's laboratory was behind the discovery in Chile, more than a decade ago, of the first giant DNA virus, dubbed [*Megavirus chilensis*]. They next identified a far larger virus of an entirely different family in 2011, dubbing it *Pandoravirus salinus*, in homage to the mythical Pandora's box that first unleashed evil on the world.

This time, they used an amoeba common to soil and water as bait to draw out a virus from a Siberian permafrost core that had been dated to 30,000 years ago.

The finding described on Monday looked like another Pandora, but it was 50 percent larger.

CHAPTER 1

"Your problem, Max, is that you take too many chances," said Brian.

Max grunted and turned his lips down in a scowl.

"Betting a week's wages when you only had a straight," said Ted, chuckling. "Max, Max, we gotta teach you to hold back, think a bit, not just go for it with no fear!"

Max gave Ted a dirty look and set his jaw in grim determination, as if their little game was a serious affair, one that his companions could never understand. "No guts, no glory," he said.

"Well now, how about another round?" asked Brian, his tone conciliatory and light.

Brian and Max were bunk mates. This was the first time that either of them had lived in the Arctic. Where Max was large, broad of shoulder and belly, Brian was short, slight of build and he always wore a cap, even indoors. Over the weeks the two men had developed a friendship as Brian enjoyed listening to Max's hunting stories and was good at explaining things about their work in a way that Max could easily understand.

Just then Evan walked in and everyone's demeanor changed. "We need to get going," he announced.

"Are you sure this is a good idea? I mean, do you think the weather will hold?" said Ted. Max didn't like Ted at all as he thought that he was too full of himself, always bragging about all his experience. Asking this kind of question was just another way of showing off.

"I do," said Evan, looking at his watch. "I think we've got a good four hours. Let's suit up and get in the bird. I want to take off in the next fifteen minutes if possible."

Max was already in his boots and warm jumpsuit, though he was wearing only a thermal shirt underneath. He reached for his thick pullover sweater, and then donned his heavy overcoat. It was bright red and had several thick bands of light-reflective material sewn into it. He didn't zip it up yet—there would be time to do that while they were in the air. As Brian and Ted re-appeared, also suited up, Max grabbed his shotgun and the case of tranquilizer darts.

Soon all four were airborne, headed for the site where they would be taking yet another ice core sample. "There's a storm on the way, but I'm confident we've got a few hours," Evan repeated to the crew in a loud voice, speaking over the sound of the helicopter blades chopping through the frigid air. He was both the pilot and the team leader. "Riesig-Alaska identified another part of Laptev Bay, near the shore, and they want a few samples from the permafrost before they decide if they will want to poke any further holes."

Before he got this job, Max had no idea how complicated oil exploration was. He had grown up in

Texas, but somehow he had never thought much about what went on before gasoline magically showed up at the local gas station, all ready to be pumped into his big black pick-up truck. After being hired by Riesigoil, however, he had undergone some training and was learning a lot from the geoscientists with whom he lived for weeks at a time in a barracks up in the Arctic. They used sound wave equipment to explore the layers under the ground, took samples, and sent all of the information to the larger base in Alaska.

Riesigoil geologists then employed 3D visualization techniques to identify areas that might harbor oil and natural gas underneath. Once potentially promising areas were identified, exploratory wells were dug, and later, if all went well, they would dig a bigger well. But even then, Max's colleagues had explained, even after all the testing and modeling, the chances of hitting a good source of oil were still only about 1 in 5. It was a long, expensive pursuit, and one that took years before any profits could be made.

Max learned these things more out of idle curiosity than anything else. Unlike most of the people in his barracks, Max had not been recruited because of his years of schooling and experience, but rather because of his hunting skills. Growing up on a ranch in the Texas hill country, Max had gone hunting from the time he was quite young, maybe six or seven years old, and it was what he loved to do most in the world. His father had also been a big hunter, as had his uncle, and he had fond memories of the long road trips they would take down to South Texas, whenever they could snag a week or two of vacation, to hunt for turkeys, feral hogs (his uncle's favorite) and deer.

On the night stand by his bunk Max kept a small framed photograph that his father had taken of him with his boot propped on the hind quarters of the first buck he had ever shot, its full crown almost larger than he was. The rush of adrenaline he had felt when he first spotted the buck in his binoculars had made his hands tremble. On previous occasions, trembling hands had led to missed shots and his quarry, thus alerted, had fled. But this time he had managed to calm himself down, and his shot had been true. After that, there had been no stopping him.

Max's friends from high school had teased him, saying that he would never get a good-paying job by pursuing his hobby. He had worked as a truck driver for a few years, but he tired of the road and longed for time off so he could get a chance to go hunting. Then one day he had seen an ad in the newspaper for an experienced hunter, and he had applied online that same evening, attaching dozens of photos of large prey that he had felled. It was the only way he could think of to impress the people who might otherwise frown at his meager work experience.

The job meant that he would have to live way up north in the Arctic for a few months of the year, but he would make enough money during that time that he could afford to take the rest of the year off and spend lots of time hunting. So far, to his dismay, being a bear hazer at Riesigoil had been much more boring than he had expected. Protecting the workers from polar bears had sounded like a lot of fun, but it had turned out to be more like just babysitting the workers while he held a toy shotgun in his hands. Still, whenever he got too frustrated by the tediousness of the endless expanse of ice, he reminded himself of the months of hunting that lay ahead, and that generally cheered him.

"The machinery's already set up there? Everything's ready to go?" asked Brian, his voice cracking as he strained to be heard over the loud stuttering of the helicopter. He was referring to the drilling equipment they would need to use to be able to remove the ice core samples. Sometimes they were required to spend extra time setting up all of the equipment, but often it was another team that identified the area and prepared it for their team.

Since they wanted samples from depths greater than 30 meters, they would need to use specialized drills that hung on cables. The drills could be electromechanical, or electrothermal, Brian had explained to Max earlier that week. Thus Max now knew that, in Brian's opinion, electrothermal drills were not as consistent and were to be avoided if possible.

"You bet," said Evan, consulting his instruments. "They have it all set for us. We should be able to get in and out in about two hours."

As they gained altitude, Max, who was sitting by a window, looked out and saw gray everywhere: the sky above, the ice below, and everything in between. The entire landscape, as far as the eye could see, was varying shades of unbroken gray. He was certain that whatever other faults it might have, Texas never had this much gray.

The ride was a short one, and within fifteen minutes, the four men had reached the site where the drilling equipment stood waiting for them. Evan put the helicopter down and soon they were outside, feeling the cold wind biting their exposed faces. Max walked over with Brian, who was wearing a bright red knit cap, and watched him as he inspected the long, cylindrical drill bit which was connected to a slender cable that would soon suspend the drill shaft as it made its way down into the hole. On the end of the drill bit Brian showed Max the four carbide teeth that would cut into the ice, shaving layer after layer as it penetrated downward.

"See these two barrels there?" Brian asked.

Max peered in and saw an inner one and an outer one.

"That motor you see there," Brian said, indicating with his gloved finger, "is attached to the inner one and that's what makes it rotate."

Max peered at the inside of the barrel of the inner core and saw the threads which spiraled up and around the inside. "What are them stringy things there for?" he asked.

"Those are called 'threads' and they serve to remove the ice chips that get freed by the carbide teeth, you see. That helps to keep the chips from getting in the way of the tip of the drill," explained Brian.

Max sauntered back toward the metallic bird, his shotgun slung carelessly over his shoulder and saw Evan cast another uneasy glance toward the west where an even darker patch of gray sky now loomed.

"Let's try to finish this one quickly and get back out of here," Evan said, his shoulders held stiffly against the wind which was beginning to pick up. The three men got busy with the equipment and began the procedure of extracting the ice core sample while Max loaded his shotgun and calmly began scanning the horizon.

"Aren't you going to use binoculars?" asked Ted. In his late forties, Ted was the oldest of the bunch, and already graying at the temples. In Max's opinion, besides being a know-it-all, Ted worried too much, especially about things which were none of his business.

"Nah," said Max, not deigning to glance in Ted's direction. "We ain't seen a single one of them in all the times I've been out here. Don't see why one of 'em would show up now."

Ted and Evan exchanged uneasy looks, but neither said anything. Max was the one with the shotgun. Besides, they needed to concentrate on the task at hand.

As they worked, Max paced around the men, walking slowly in a circle and scanning the horizon. There was nothing but gray on all sides. Occasionally he would stop and watch the men for a while. The noisy drill was steadily spewing up tiny bits and chunks of shredded ice which formed a growing mound that would have been quite nice for snow cones.

The drill shaft had disappeared fairly soon after drilling had begun, and now just the cable could be seen, snaking over and into the ever deepening hole. After a few minutes Max would begin pacing again, stopping every now and then to look at the storm and gauge its progression. Gusts of wind were increasing in frequency, but the menacing dark clouds looked like they would indeed not make their appearance until later in the afternoon.

After about an hour, Brian signaled that the drill had reached the location from which they wanted to extract the core sample, and they began the reverse drilling operations to bring it up to the surface. The first few times Max had seen an ice-core being extracted, he had been quite interested. They had removed the long pole-like structure, thinner than his wrist, and wrapped it carefully and quickly, hermetically sealing it in one single chunk for later analysis. Once it was sealed in plastic, they would pack it in Styrofoam and packing bubbles to protect it. This was the most precarious part of the entire operation. The sample needed to remain intact in order for the lab techs back at the barracks to be able to analyze it properly. It was a delicate operation, but the men made it seem fairly easy. Max wasn't fooled, though. Hunting had taught him that it took many months of practice before things looked easy.

The men worked for another fifty minutes to bring the sample up. As the drill bore finally re-appeared, everyone, including Max, watched in fascination. They lowered the shaft slightly and began to gently eject the sample from the inner casing of the drill. First the tip, then agonizingly slowly, the rest of the crystalline core sample began to gently slide out as the men waited, plastic bag and Styrofoam at the ready. The roar came at the worst possible moment, just as the last part of the ice-core sample had emerged into the air.

Max's heart raced as he cocked his shotgun and whirled toward the sound. He sighted his prey and immediately took aim, but he didn't pull the trigger yet. He had hoped and dreamed of just such a moment for so many weeks. Now his pent-up adrenaline raced through his veins. He took a deep breath, steadying himself.

The bear stopped advancing and reared up on its hind legs. It was an enormous beast, all the more fearsome as it towered over them, its keen black eyes now more than twelve feet above the ice. Slowly swiveling its head, the bear surveyed the group, as if pondering which one of the men it should attack first. Honing in on Brian, clearly the smallest of the crew members, it flared its nostrils and opened its large mouth in a rumbling growl, revealing four long incisors, each capable of inflicting mortal wounds.

Max followed the bear's gaze and saw Brian, who had been reaching for the fragile ice core sample to wrap it in the plastic bag, flinch violently at the sound of the menacing growl, and then lose his purchase on a slick patch of ice.

All of the Arctic workers had undergone long hours of safety training in case of bear attacks, which had included pictures of bears. But, from experience, Max knew there simply was no substitute for having the live, hulking animal, right there.

Trying to recover his balance, Brian staggered forward, flailing wildly with his arms. Both Evan and Ted tried to catch Brian as he tottered, but their thick suits and the slippery ice made them clumsy. Before they could catch him, Brian slammed into the ice core sample which had been hanging perilously on the edge of the drill shaft. The plug of ice broke free and clattered to the ground unceremoniously, fracturing and sending splinters of ice, like tiny darts, into the exposed faces of the men.

"What are you waiting for? Shoot it!" Ted yelled at Max.

Max, however, paused for another moment. It was one of the greatest moments of his life and he was relishing the inimitable experience. The bear got back down on all four legs and began loping toward the men. Max's entire body tingled as he tracked it. Then, in one swift motion, he pulled the trigger and shot several times, sending four quivering darts into the flesh of the white bear. He felt a momentary pang of regret that he was not using real bullets, but he would still have a good story to tell his peers when he got back to Texas.

As he watched the big animal topple clumsily down onto the ice, the skin on the back of Max's neck pricked up, a hunter's sixth sense, and he whirled in time to see a second bear bounding toward the group of men. It was about forty five degrees to the right of the one that was still struggling, shaking its head as if bewildered.

"Get down," Max barked at his companions, taking a few quick steps to position himself between the bear and the other men. He cocked his shotgun, more thrilled than afraid, and ignoring the frightened howls of his companions, he fired three times. The injections hit the big animal squarely on the shoulder, side and hip. The bear's pace did not seem to slow. Max stood his ground, firing several more well-placed shots. He knew that the amount of tranquilizer in each dart was more than enough to kill a man, and that their combined force would soon immobilize the bear.

The colossal mass of white fur, saber claws and sharp teeth swerved and slipped as it finally went down, then skidded, reaching out its large paw to swipe at Max. The claws of the giant animal rasped against Max's leg and tore at his suit, even as the bear's eyes rolled skyward and its head struck the ice with a large thump. Thirty feet away, the first bear also lay unconscious.

Max quickly scanned the horizon, turning his head carefully to his left in a full circle to ascertain that there were no other surprises lurking. All was clear.

He bent over and casually inspected his pants. They were torn in several places, but no further harm had been done. Then he turned and registered that his companions were cursing, and that the ice core sample lay shattered in six or seven large chunks.

"Let's take it anyway," shouted Evan. The winds were beginning to blow even harder, and white crystals, pieces of shattered core as well as blowing snow, covered all of the men, dusting their hair, faces and bright coats. With gloved hands and hunched backs they scooped up the lopsided cylindrical chunks of ice and placed them in the bag. They did not bother with the Styrofoam or packing bubbles as there was no longer any need to take precautions not to break it.

"Let's get out of here," yelled Evan and soon they had mounted the helicopter and were on their way back to the camp.

"What the hell happened?" demanded Ted as soon as they were in the air. The storm was definitely closer now, and everyone was obviously nervous to get back to the shelter of their barracks as soon as possible.

"What?" said Max, vexed that none of them, not even Brian, had thanked him for saving their lives. And now here was Ted interrogating him. Well, he certainly wasn't going to let some old dude tell him how he should have handled the situation. He was the only one who had kept his cool in the face of danger instead of panicking like sissies.

Ted rolled his eyes. "The *bears*, man, what the hell was that about?"

Max shrugged. It was clear that Ted was just being a nervous worrywart again. Perhaps that was why he had so much gray hair even though he wasn't fifty years old yet.

The adrenaline from Max's encounter with the polar bears had dissipated quickly. That was the trouble with hunting. It used to be that a good kill would create a euphoria that would last for the rest of the day. Now he got about ten minutes of that high feeling, and soon he was completely back to normal. He wondered if it was because he had been hunting for so long, or if it was an age thing, yet one more trick his older body had learned to play on him. Or perhaps it was because, deep down, he knew he had not actually killed the bears, only immobilized them temporarily.

"Why did you take so long to shoot them?" snapped Ted, his jaw flexing.

Max shot him a dirty look. "I didn't take that long. Y'all were never in any real danger. I wanted to be sure the big guy got close enough that I could get him good. And I did."

"And the second bear?" asked Evan.

Great. They were ganging up on him now. Well, bring it on, thought Max. He could handle these wimps. He looked straight ahead and shrugged again. "What of it? I got him good too, didn't I?" Then he turned back toward the window, angling his shoulder as a barrier against the other men.

Ted looked at Evan who, almost imperceptibly, shook his head. Then, after quickly glancing in his mirror to be sure that Max wasn't looking, Evan held his hand slightly aloft, as if supporting an invisible pen. Ted gave a single nod. They would write up Max's behavior when they returned to the barracks.

Brian flushed as he observed the interaction, feeling a pang of guilt for not intervening on behalf of his friend. After all, Max was doing his job as he understood it. And polar bears *were* incredibly difficult to spot since their fur was as translucent as ice. So it wasn't that surprising that the bears had snuck up on them.

Then the memory of the gargantuan bears, the first of which seemed to have locked eyes with him, came crashing back, paralyzing him once again with fear. Maybe it wasn't Max's fault for not descrying the bears sooner, but he really had erred in not shooting them earlier. Brian's eyes drifted to the window where they became snagged in the ponderous clouds and escalating winds that blew away the last vestiges of his contrition.

Back in the barracks, the men doffed their outerwear and dried off. A few minutes later Evan radioed mission control to report the incident, as Riesigoil protocol dictated.

"Two bears? That's highly unusual," said the static-filled voice of their supervisor.

She said something else after that, but after a few seconds of loud crackling sounds, the connection was lost. The storm that had been brewing on the horizon for the last several hours, growing ever larger and darker, now sank its fangs into the land. For two solid days the incessant winds howled and hail and snow pelted relentlessly on the tin roof of the small barracks, sounding as if the Arctic was waging a war with them, shelling their camp mercilessly.

No one could go outside. Communication satellites were blocked by the thick, impenetrable gray clouds. No one could reach the outside world. No one could hear their cries for help. No one would ever forget the horror of the events that occurred inside.

CHAPTER 2

"We are still in the early stages of exploring the area," said Angela. She registered Oscar's inquisitive look and decided it would be best to start from the beginning.

"Before oil is pumped, there's quite a long process, which can take several years. One of the first steps is to take ice core samples, ascertain conditions, and analyze all of the geological data to try to find the areas which are most conducive to supplying oil. There are lots of other steps too, especially in the Arctic. We have to make sure that we are analyzing the environment and taking measures to protect it. We've got to make sure that we can contain and clean up any spills and that we're not looking to drill in an area that turns out to be the one and only breeding ground for some rare Arctic bird or something."

Although Angela had not visited with Oscar in several years, their friendship went back to their college days. They had lived in the same dorm, albeit on separate floors, and their roommates had dated. They had since kept in touch, through their mutual friends, and had both ended up in Houston. Oscar had married, divorced, and married again. Angela did not know his second wife, but she had maintained her connection to him through occasional phone calls, and now she felt comfortable sitting in his large office and telling her story as it ought to be told.

"After we take the ice core samples, we dig exploratory wells to see if there is any oil there, then we examine its quality and measure how extensive the oil field seems to be. Sometimes the oil is embedded in rocks. It's as if the rocks were giant sponges and the oil was trapped in all the spaces in between. In order to get the rocks to release the oil, we have to resort to different techniques such as using dynamite to get it to pool and then flow into the well bore…but, all of that's beside the point for this discussion. What's important here is that our team was only beginning to assess the area and make initial estimates of where and how deep to drill."

Oscar nodded and took a sip of his coffee, and as he did so, Angela's eyes were drawn to his thin lips. It was almost as if he didn't have lips at all, like a Muppet. And then there was his unibrow. She had to avert her eyes to keep from smiling as she remembered how all those years ago he had reminded her of Bert from Sesame Street. He had a long, thin face, already balding in his early twenties. Fortunately, in his older age he had gained a little weight and grown a goatee, both of which certainly helped attenuate the resemblance.

Angela forced herself to think about something else. She was here on pressing business. And Oscar was a busy man, after all. He was president of the Houston branch of the University of Texas, and she appreciated the fact that he was not rushing her.

"As I'm sure you can imagine, much of the Arctic has been portioned or claimed by different countries and companies. So we were in an area that our company owns, up in the Laptev Bay area. We had a small group of workers there, maybe fifteen people. All of them were experienced, mind you. There was a barracks that we built for the team. This part of the world is basically inaccessible for nine months of the year, so we get our teams out there as soon as we possibly can in late May, and they work for three solid months, living in the barracks, weathering any storms that may spring up. At the end of August we pull them out."

Oscar pulled at his chin with its ring of mostly gray hair, thinking. He reached for the map of the Arctic that Angela had brought to the meeting and searched. "So they were right about here," he said, now pointing with his finger. It was on the northern border of Siberia. "I don't know much about oil and gas exploration, but of course everyone knows that Siberia has a lot of these natural resources."

"That's right. And like I said, Riesigoil is only one of many players up there. A few days ago the team, a small group of men, apparently went out to take some ice core samples of an area we were looking into. Routine stuff. Now, when ice core samples are taken, there is a fairly strict procedure that must be adhered to. We share the data with major research organizations that are investigating climate change and in general trying to decipher how the world looked millions of years ago. In order to preserve the ice core samples, they are wrapped carefully as soon as they emerge, and maintained at a temperature of -15°C. It's all standard procedure, you understand."

"Yes," said Oscar, pressing his flat lips together.

"The samples are then transported back to the barracks where there are labs set up for analysis. Samples are normally kept hermetically sealed, isolated from human contact or from contact with the atmosphere because the investigative teams want to also be able to study environmental and atmospheric conditions that were present on earth when these ice layers were first formed, and these parameters cannot be assessed if the samples get contaminated."

"That's right. I remember studying that a long time ago," said Oscar with a wink. They often joked about how long ago college had been.

"It was something about how ice layers formed as the snow fell, year after year, accumulating and trapping small bubbles of air and anything that was present in the air at the time."

"Yes," said Angela. "And besides the actual chemical makeup of the air, including how much carbon dioxide, methane and other gasses it had, scientists can also discover what else was floating around in the atmosphere, including ash, pollen and even microorganisms. After thousands of years of continually adding blanket upon blanket of snow and ice, these layers became more and more compact, sinking deeper and deeper. This sample these men took that day, though, was from the permafrost, which is a thick layer of soil that has not thawed in thousands of years. It was from deep down, so we know it's old, but it wasn't just ice, which is pretty much sterile."

"And something went wrong?" asked Oscar.

Angela nodded gravely and crossed her legs. Something had gone terribly wrong. Pandemonium had struck that remote little corner of the world and lives had been lost. That is what had brought her to this precipitous visit with her old friend.

"Bingo. As a safety precaution, Riesigoil, and pretty much every exploration company that I know of, employs a bear hazer—a sharpshooter with a modified shotgun that holds tranquilizer darts—to protect the team, just in case there is unwelcome company you know. Polar bears aren't exactly the friendliest creatures around," she said with a wry smile. "This particular team was just four men, and they had come by helicopter to the site. Of course, helicopter pilots always check the weather carefully before making a flight, and according to the log books we found, the forecast had been acceptable. They knew that there was a storm on the way, but they felt certain that they could get back to base camp before it arrived. And they did manage to do just that. But they experienced a series of unfortunate events."

Angela consulted her notes, wanting to be sure that she did not omit any details. It was important to her company to secure Oscar's promise to help immediately, and she needed to impress upon him the seriousness and precariousness of the situation.

"First, not one, but two bears showed up. Usually polar bears, especially the males, are solitary creatures and you rarely, if ever, see two at a time. Maybe it was the fact that it was the beginning of summer and so the ice was melting. Maybe the bears were hungrier after the winter—I don't know. The fact is that while the bear hazer was dealing with the first one, the second one got too close to the group and managed to scare the men before the hazer got both bears tranquilized. According to the pilot's notes, a guy named Evan Shapiro, the bear hazer had ample opportunity and should have taken the bears out before they got that close to the team. The hazer, a guy by the name of Max Maldonado, obviously disagrees with Shapiro's report. Max is a big hunter and did not think that there was any risk, but in any case, I would say this was their first mistake."

"Wow, you never really hear of polar bear attacks. That's pretty scary."

"Yes, well, I can't even imagine. Anyway, the reason this is important is because since the team came under a perceived and immediate threat, they lost focus of what they were doing with the ice core sample that they were just removing from the well, and before they could get it properly wrapped, they dropped it and it shattered on the ice. This turned out to be the second mistake."

Oscar grimaced.

"The workers were pretty upset of course, but they decided to rescue the pieces, and labeled them as 'contaminated' but figured that the lab might still learn something, so they transported them back to the barracks. Now we know that this was another grave mistake, and perhaps it was the biggest one of them all.

"A few hours after they returned to the barracks, all four of the individuals who had been at the drill site, including the hazer, began to develop flu-like symptoms. The infection advanced quickly, and in three of the four people, it developed into hemorrhagic fever."

At this point in her narrative, Angela stopped and swallowed. The gruesome images were seared into her mind. She had never met the men, but she regretted the loss of life, especially when it had been so sudden and obviously painful.

She had an uncle who had been an engineer and had died when a unit exploded at the refinery where he worked in Texas City ten years ago. As with all accidents, there had been multiple causes and compounded human errors. A valve had accidentally gotten stuck in the "open" position, and someone else had not followed safety procedures. He had driven a pickup truck, parked it too close to the unit, and left the motor idling. Forensic analysts said that a spark from the engine had ignited the leaking gas, killing both her uncle and the truck driver. Angela had been a senior in college at the time, and after the funeral she had decided to make health and safety her career.

"We lost two of the men who were part of the exploration team that day," she said, her voice somber.

"The hazer?" asked Oscar.

"He lived, as did one other worker, an older man named Ted. But that's not all. Within a day, the lab technicians who were working in the barracks and had begun to examine the ice core sample also became ill, and several of them passed away too. Meanwhile, since everyone up there in the barracks lives in close quarters, several more workers became ill and pretty soon there was a full-blown epidemic in the little building."

"They didn't radio for help?"

"They tried," said Angela, looking out of the window. The warm Houston day was fine and a huge, light blue sky hung over the buildings. Just a block away she could see the dark green tree tops peeking out from Hermann Park.

The UT Medical School building was sleek and modern and had a funny smell. When Oscar had met her downstairs he had given her a brief tour of the building. She had wrinkled her nose at the smell and he had explained that it was due to the autoclaves, which were the sterilization ovens that were located on each of the different levels. In any case, the peaceful scene around her could not be more different from the one the men in the Laptev Bay barracks had experienced.

"They tried to call for help, but the storm knocked out communications for two days. That's not unusual, even at this time of the year, but normally there isn't an epidemic to deal with."

"And the bodies?"

"They burned most of them, fearing the contagion. As soon as we received the distress calls, we immediately sent in doctors to try to contain the situation. Naturally, we hadn't realized how desperate the situation had become, but when the doctors saw the gravity of the circumstances, they decided to close the barracks and airlift everyone out. They brought them here to Houston for hospitalization—this was just a few days ago, and we've managed to keep it out of the news so far. We certainly don't need another Ebola scare, and we don't want to make any statements to the press until we understand what we are dealing with. We've managed to keep the patients in quarantine, and we got some tissue samples analyzed. So far, all we know is that the contagion seems to be a large virus, one of those megaviruses that have been found in different places around the world in inhospitable environments. This is a new one that has never been encountered before. It's being called the Laptev hemorrhagic fever virus, or Laptev HFV."

"And you want the university to help with the research?" asked Oscar.

Angela arched an eyebrow as if to say, Duh! Hello! Why else would I be telling you this?

Oscar lowered his head. "Yes, of course," he said softly. "We'll be happy to do what we can to help."

"Riesigoil, will, of course, donate all of the supplies, and provide ample funding for the research. We need to get to the bottom of this as soon as possible. We certainly don't want to lose any more of our people."

"Right," said Oscar. "Your company has always been generous with the university." It was a true statement, and the way he said it told Angela that he had no trouble at all in admitting it. This was, after all, Houston, the city with quite possibly the largest concentration of engineers per capita in the world. The big oil and chemical companies were generous in their funding of the universities across the state, and any good university president was well aware of this fact.

"There is one other thing you should know. For now, all drilling and exploration has been halted in that area, of course."

Oscar looked at Angela, his bushy eyebrow now one long line across the top of his forehead. "But it can't remain that way," he said.

"Unfortunately, we only have three months of the year that we can work up there. The Arctic contains a vast amount of oil and gas—enough to make North America energy independent for the foreseeable future. We've finally obtained the permits we need to begin drilling, and we've invested billions of dollars and moved tons of equipment up there. My CEO tells me that the shareholders will not take kindly to matters if we have to report back that we let an entire season go by without further exploration, and then we cannot do anything for another nine months while the winter rages on."

"I understand. We will work quickly on this investigation. We're very fortunate to have the former head of the CDC, Dr. Rhonda Bentley, leading the Infectious Diseases department. I'll inform her of this decision and I'm sure she'll get a team right on it," said Oscar.

Angela sighed imperceptibly with relief. It was the answer she had been hoping to receive, given the urgency of the issue for her company. She would visit her CEO, Stan Sundback, as soon as she returned to her office and let him know.

CHAPTER 3

"Can I play with Opus? Pretty please!"

Molly was so focused that she didn't glance up from her laptop. She was busy trying to finish writing the essay for her anthropology class, 'Pre-humans in the Iberian Peninsula'. She was fascinated with the subject and had found some interesting journal articles in the last few days using the new online database that the library had acquired. In one of the articles she was reading how there seemed to be direct evidence that Neanderthals and modern humans had coincided, inhabiting caves only a mile apart, for more than 5,000 years, in northern Spain. In another more ancient cave they had discovered 17 skulls with Neanderthal-like features which were thought to be over 30,000 years old.

It was so fascinating that she was seriously thinking of changing her major from Psychology to Anthropology. How she wished she could go there and be a part of the archaeological discovery teams. Maybe she would do a Master's degree in Anthro? Maybe she could apply for an NSF grant once she graduated next year…

"Come on, Moll-Moll!" said her brother, interrupting her thoughts. "I'll just have him out for a little bit. I promise!"

"*Hmm*? Yeah, sure, go ahead," she said distractedly. Her younger brother loved the little mouse she had brought home one day from the laboratory animal care facility. She worked there part-time, 10-20 hours per week, cleaning the cages and feeding the mice. The mice were bred for all kinds of experiments, and although some were more intrusive tests, requiring the mice to receive injections or grow tumors which could be studied to find anti-cancer drugs, many mice were used for behavioral studies or as control mice for the tumor studies, which required nothing more of them than to live normal healthy lives so they could be used for comparison to the others. These were the mice she usually cared for.

One day about three weeks ago, one of the graduate students, Kevin, had told her about Opus, though the mouse had not yet been baptized as such. Molly really liked Kevin. It wasn't just that he was probably closely related to Channing Tatum, as evidenced by his green eyes and gorgeous smile. It was because even though he was obviously busy and had tons of friends who were constantly contacting him on his cell phone, he still made time to explain things and teach her things, unlike the other technicians, some of whom were just plain nasty.

The researchers in the department that studied HIV/AIDS, he explained, were performing a non-intrusive study to see how long it took for the mice to wake up from anesthesia. Sometimes they did benign tests like this to see if there was any way to make this process more tolerable for the little mice. They had tried different methods for waking them, and they had found that the colder the mice were, the more lethal the anesthesia was. So they were trying different methods for keeping the mice warm to see if they could help the mice emerge more healthily from the somniferous effect of the anesthetic.

"We kept him under an electric blanked for several hours afterwards, you see," explained Kevin. "Otherwise he would be too cold and never wake up."

"Aw, he doesn't like being a little penguin!" she exclaimed, obviously upset and reaching out a finger to stroke the soft white fur.

"Well, that's why we were trying to keep him warm," he said, flashing her that irresistible smile with little dimples in his cheeks. "We used to just leave the mice to wake up on their own, but this latest test confirmed that if we artificially maintained the mice at a constant 37 degrees Celsius, and allowed them to wake up slowly, they do much better."

Molly listened enraptured as he explained that the procedure had worked and the mouse was fine, but now, lab protocol dictated, he could not be a part of any further studies, since mice could not be re-used, and once mice had left the kennels where they were kept and had been mixed with other mice, they were not supposed to be returned to their original homes. It was a shame to put him down when he was otherwise healthy, but those were the rules.

"So, there's nothing wrong with him?" Molly inquired, hoping she didn't appear stupid.

"Nothing at all. Now that he's warmed up and woken up, he's perfectly fine. Our test worked and now we know that it's better to wake the mice up that way. So he served his purpose and future anesthetized mice will have an easier time coming out of it."

Molly pictured an incubator with a long, two inch wide electric blanket and the mice all lying down in a long row, their tiny little heads, feet and tails peeking out from top and bottom of the blanket as they slowly recovered from the anesthesia. Or maybe it would be like a sauna, or a resort for mice, all nice and cozy and warm. Perhaps some of them would wake up earlier than the others and start crawling around? Would the researchers also put food and water in there for the early risers? She shook her head at her own silly thinking and took the mouse gently from Kevin. It stretched and gave a small yawn, which made her smile. "So you're sure there's nothing unusual about him?" she repeated. "No built-in tumors, no aneurism time bombs or anything?"

Kevin's brow furrowed and he looked in mock concentration, then he brightened. "He was sterilized as a pup, but nothing else. Off you go, little guy," he said, taking the mouse back from Molly's hand.

Just then Tammy, one of the technicians whom Molly really disliked, entered the room.

"Oh, Kevin, there you are," she said in a breathy voice, batting her pretty blue eyes at him before turning and giving Molly a quick up and down look that was both assessing and dismissive.

Molly took a step back from Kevin even though there was no reason for her to do so—they were doing nothing wrong. But somehow she always felt intimidated by Tammy with her impeccable blonde hair and attractive long eyelashes which she heavily accentuated. Molly seemed to always forget about wearing make-up until she came in contact with someone like Tammy who obviously spent an inordinate amount of time on her appearance.

"Kevin, I need you to come take a look at a situation we have in C8," Tammy cooed.

Molly noticed that there was no 'please' or 'when you have time.' Tammy assumed that if he was with Molly it was not important. All pretty girls seemed to think that what they had to say to someone like Kevin was much more interesting than whatever she would have to say, and the realization made a small blush creep over Molly's face.

"Um," said Kevin, still holding the mouse.

"I can take him," said Molly reaching for the mouse. "I have an empty cage back in C12."

"But the mice aren't supposed to mix."

"It's all right," she said quickly. "I've got a cage that's been cleaned and it's separate from the others. I'll just keep him there for a few hours and then I'll take him to the Waiting Room if you want."

Kevin hesitated.

"Kevin," said Tammy, drawing out the syllables in his name. She was clearly becoming impatient. She strutted over to him and handed him a notebook. "Come on. I need to show this to you now."

Kevin glanced at the notebook and then turned back toward Molly. "Okay, I guess that's fine, but please don't forget to take him to the Waiting Room later. You'll remember?"

"Of course," said Molly, accepting the mouse and turning away from Tammy. After Kevin and Tammy left, she took the little guy by the scruff of his neck to place him in a carrying cage which she would use to transport him back to Room C12, the room in the vivarium where she worked. Later that afternoon she would take him to the room they had euphemistically nicknamed the 'Waiting Room', which was at the far end of the building. There she would place him in a larger cage and the mouse would be mixed with all of the other mice that could no longer be used. These "expended" mice were stored together and had one last chance to enjoy themselves, romping and playing with their peers, before they were sent to be sacrificed painlessly.

Room C12 was much like room C8, where Kevin had gone with Tammy, and all of the other mice storage rooms of the vivarium. It was a sterile-looking room, with white walls, a white ceiling embedded with two long rows of fluorescent lights. The floor and walls were a light tan color and they were made of a special polyurethane resin which ensured that there were no cracks or crevices where bacteria could possibly hide. A slightly musty smell, mixed with the scent of the furry animal bodies filled the air, though Molly rarely ever noticed it except when she had not been in the room for a long time. Stainless steel racks on wheels were lined up in rows, and the nesting cages were placed side-by-side on these racks.

The nesting cages were not too different from the hamster cage she had had when she was younger: they were transparent plastic bins, lined with a couple of inches of bedding and litter material, and over the top of each bin was an angled metallic rack which supported a water bottle and a tray of food so that the rodents could help themselves as they pleased. Brightly colored index cards fit into a slot on the front of the cage, and these were labeled with the type of mice found in the cage, their birth dates (the mice were mostly siblings of each other, though the males were kept separate from the females) and any other relevant information.

Each nesting cage held up to six mice. Technically the mice from different nesting cages were not supposed to mix with each other, Molly knew, but occasionally, when she was sure no one would find out, Molly did let the mice she cared for visit with one another. Mice were social creatures, she reasoned, and as long as she didn't get them mixed up, there certainly was no harm in letting them be gregarious.

Besides, since the mice in C12 were control mice, it was not like they could contaminate each other with some dreadful disease. No, these were the "normal" mice, healthy and happy, to be used for comparison when researchers did experiments on the other mice from other rooms, so letting them have a little companionable time was of no consequence whatsoever. Still, in her heart of hearts, Molly knew that the researchers would not approve, so she kept her little secret to herself.

Molly walked to the correct rack and found the shelf and the empty cage where she could lodge the mouse for a few hours while she had lunch. Just before placing him in the cage, she examined him once more and he looked up at her with his perfectly round eyes and cute ears which laid back in complete trust. Although she didn't usually pay much attention to individual mice, at that moment she felt a pang of regret and realized that she didn't want to surrender the little guy to be put down. It simply wasn't fair.

Instead of placing him in the cage, she walked over to the desk in the corner of the room and released him on the surface. She watched him sniff around, crawling over a pencil and nibbling on the corner of her notepad. Then something spooked him and he ran back to her gloved hand, sheltering in her curved palm. Her little penguin needed her.

She held him up, allowing him to crouch in her palm and examined him closely. He wasn't perfectly white—there was a small light-brown patch on his left leg, which made it almost look like he was wearing a boot. Again he stared up at her with dark, trusting eyes that looked like perfect little black marbles.

"Aw, poor little thing," she said softly, and looked furtively around to be sure that she was completely alone. She was. Without thinking too much about what she was doing, she slipped the mouse into the pocket of her lab coat and then strode out of the brightly lit animal room and walked across the hall to the changing room.

As she entered, her eyes swept over the rows of lockers where people stored their lab coats, backpacks and jackets. There were a couple of benches on one end, and a sink with strong-smelling antiseptic soap in the corner. The room was empty. Her heart racing, she strode to her locker and yanked it open. With quivering hands she surreptitiously withdrew the little mouse from her lab coat pocket and slid it into a mesh pouch inside her backpack. Then she quickly zipped everything shut.

"Hey, Molly, how's it going?" said Kevin.

Molly's hand jerked and she nearly dropped the backpack, but she recovered quickly and hung it on its hook. She had not heard him enter the changing room.

"Good," she said, her voice squeaking slightly. She stuck her head back into the locker to cover her reddening face and pretended to be fiddling with her backpack.

"Did you get a chance to take that mouse to the Waiting Room?"

"I..." she said, and then cleared her throat and started again. "I put him in the cage back in C12 for a bit, but I'll take him down to the other room right after lunch," she said, trying to sound casual, and began unbuttoning her lab coat. "I'm meeting someone right now but I'll be back right afterwards, if that's okay?"

Even as she spoke she was making plans about what she would say if he asked to see the mouse now. How would she explain that it was not in the cage where she had said that she would place it? Could she maybe hold up a different mouse and say it was him? Would Kevin be able to tell that mouse apart from the others? Most likely he would not, unless he too had noticed the little spot on the mouse's leg.

"Okay, I guess that's cool," he said, his gaze darting sideways. He removed his lab coat and pulled his locker open. Then he fished his cell phone out of his pocket and began scrolling through it. "Listen," he said, his eyes meeting hers. "I probably won't be back today. I've got a huge paper due tomorrow. So, see you the day after?"

"Yeah," she said, her voice quavering annoyingly. She had to regain control of herself. She willed her arms not to tremble as she reached for her backpack and lifted it off its hook. She had already removed her lab coat and tossed her gloves in the bin.

"No problem. Good luck on that essay!" she said swiftly. Normally she would have been tempted to linger—Kevin was so hot—but today she knew that her face would betray her if she tarried even a minute longer. She slid her backpack gingerly onto her shoulder and hurried toward the door. As she pushed it open she met Tammy—was she following Kevin? Tammy gave her the usual once-over, but Molly just kept going. She could not risk that her little captive would make a noise or do something to give them away.

At home she told her mother the mouse story. "I'm thinking of calling him 'Penguin' " she said.

"Well, if he's a penguin, then I think Opus would be a better name," said her mother, tenderly petting their new little friend. When she saw Molly's puzzled look, she added, "Bloom County. It was a comic strip that I used to follow when I was your age. There was a penguin named Opus and he was great."

At first Opus had slept in her canary's old cage, since her mom had donated the hamster cage to Goodwill. But in just a few days her little penguin was part of the family, being set free more and more often. Her cat, which her mother had named Esmeralda because of her beautiful green eyes, had had kittens a few weeks earlier, and the whole family had been entertained, watching the tiny fur-balls when their mother allowed it for a few minutes each day. She was the kindest cat Molly had ever met. Certainly her cousins' cats were not so friendly when they had babies, but this old Esmeralda shared her motherhood freely. Soon, even little Opus was playing with the kittens, to everyone's delight. The weeks had gone by in a flash and Molly no longer worried that her small transgression of taking the mouse would ever be discovered.

Today, since it was his two month birthday and she wanted to do something special for him, Molly had taken Opus for a nice little visit to his old stomping grounds, back in the vivarium. He had ridden in her backpack, and he had behaved perfectly. It was the first time she had done something like this, and she was pleased that she had pulled it off without anyone noticing.

"Hey Moll-Moll, something's wrong here," said her brother.

"*Hmm?*" said Molly, her attention still focused on her computer screen. She had clicked on a series of Neanderthal links and was realizing that she was probably straying too far afield from the original assignment. She began closing some of the tabs, trying to make herself focus on the exam material.

"Moll-Moll, hey, looky here. This isn't Opus. You've got an imposter!"

Molly took an exasperated breath. Little brothers could be so annoying when you wanted to get some work done! How was she ever going to finish reading the articles if he kept distracting her? She really had to concentrate or she was never going to be ready for tomorrow. "What do you mean?" she asked gruffly.

"Opus has a spot on his *left* leg, doesn't he?"

Molly exhaled loudly, though her exasperation was quickly giving way to tingling pricks of fear. "Yes, you know that, Kurt, now cut it out! I've got to finish studying or I'll fail this exam!" she said, feigning annoyance to cover her anxiety.

"But this one has the spot on his *right* leg."

Molly's eyes opened wide and she felt her face flushing with apprehension. She immediately swiveled toward her little brother. "That isn't funny," she said, her voice barely above a whisper.

"I'm not joking, I swear it! Look!" said Kurt.

Molly reached for the mouse. It only took a second for her to see that her kid brother was right. She closed her eyes and shook her head in consternation. She would be in huge trouble if anyone back at the lab found out about the mess-up. They took daily counts of the mice, so at least that number would be fine because although she had taken one mouse into the vivarium, she had brought one mouse back home.

But which mouse had she brought home? And poor Opus, whose life she had preserved, would he now suddenly be in danger? Would she be able to get him back before he became the subject of some hideous experiment? The implications of her mistake pelted down on her as if she had been caught in a hail storm, one sharp whack after another smacking her on her arms and head.

She looked at her watch. Almost eight o'clock. Surely no one would be doing experiments so late at night? But there was no way for her to return to the lab at this hour of the night to make the exchange. Oh, why had she thought it was a good idea to take him back to visit his friends for the day? Why hadn't she just kept him at home? And how had he gotten mixed in with the others? She had called softly to him and he had come straight back to her. Pet rodents were really good about that. Only it wasn't him but some weird mirror-twin with the same mark on his right leg. How had she not realized her mistake then and there?

Well, there was nothing for it now. She would be sure to be the first one in room C12 tomorrow morning to rectify the mistake. One night, that's all. She would make the swap and then bring Opus straight home before her morning class. No one would ever know.

CHAPTER 4

As Sarah plodded along slowly toward the elevator for her urgent meeting with Rhonda Bentley, she had time to ruminate. The truth was that working in the pathology department under the former director of the Center for Disease Control, however glamorous that might sound, had its drawbacks. Rhonda often acted as if she still worked at the CDC. Maybe it was because she was the first African American woman to have achieved such a high position in that organization. Or maybe she was just a driven Type A personality. Whatever the reason, she thrived on challenges and was perpetually interested in investigating whatever epidemic was making headlines in the world. It didn't matter that she didn't actually do the investigating herself but rather foisted the job onto the researchers under her command.

Rhonda had intimated that she wanted to discuss "an exciting new project" for Sarah's team to study. What would it be now, Sarah wondered. Last year Rhonda had been obsessed with the Ebola outbreak, and before that she had been consumed with avian flu in the Far East. A few years earlier, it had been the typhoid epidemics that had struck the poor island countries after the summer hurricanes.

Rhonda had several high profile investigators on her team, but it seemed to Sarah that Rhonda picked on her more often than on the other investigators. Why didn't she ask Larry to drop his dengue fever research, or Chuck to cut short his latest projects on protozoan infections? Surely both of those areas were not as important as the research her team was doing on AIDS?

The elevator doors opened and Sarah limped in and pressed the large '5' button. She hated having to take the snail paced elevator up the two flights to her boss's office, but her bandaged leg gave her no other option. Fortunately she no longer needed the little tricycle contraption on which she had rested her knee for the first few weeks after her surgery. She winced as she remembered the steel post they had inserted into her ankle.

Sarah stepped out on the fifth floor and headed toward Rhonda's office. As she approached, the office administrator saw her coming and rose to help her.

"Won't you have a seat, Dr. Spallanzani? I'll let Dr. Bentley know that you've arrived. Would you care for some coffee?"

Sarah thanked her and shrugged off the niceties. She was used to being the fearless leader, not some invalid to be fussed over. Her job was to lead a team of investigators who were researching a way to combat HIV, and they had finally developed a drug which was showing promising signs in its ability to fight AIDS without the slew of nasty side-effects caused by the cocktail of drugs currently being used. Moreover, unlike the other drugs on the market, it stimulated the body to re-grow the immune cells which HIV had devastated. If clinical testing went well, Sarah and her team believed that this drug, which they had derived from aloe plants, could be affordably produced for millions of people.

In another moment Rhonda stepped out of her office and waved Sarah in.

"We've got an exciting opportunity," she said, her eyes shining. "There is a strange outbreak in the Arctic. A new virus has been identified, and I think that your team is in an ideal position for investigating it. What we're dealing with is the Laptev virus, named for the sea basin in the Arctic where the virus was discovered. Like Ebola in Africa, the Laptev virus is lethal."

As she listened, Sarah imagined that it must feel like falling in love for Rhonda each time a new project appeared on the horizon. She, however, was not excited about the idea.

"I just feel that abandoning the research that my team has been doing on AIDS just as it was on the cusp of being something really great for humanity, is not something we should do lightly," said Sarah, hoping to talk some sense into her boss.

"Believe me, I'm fully aware of the advances your team has made," Rhonda said, smiling. She spoke daggers in the tone of roses.

Sarah opened her mouth to interject, but Rhonda raised her hand, palm outward, to stop her. "I am *fully* aware," she repeated, "and what's more, I promise that as soon as we make some headway on this new deadly megavirus, we will have you back on track with your AIDS research."

Sarah pursed her lips. She was not mollified but she dared not resist. When Rhonda had first taken over as head of Infectious Disease Investigation (IDI) several years ago, she had quickly dispensed with researchers who did not want to investigate in the areas that she considered most important. It was Rhonda's prerogative and indeed, her duty, Sarah knew, to be sure that the IDI conformed to the lines of study that would bring in the most prestige and money to the university, so she understood that Rhonda was not merely being tyrannical with her directives. Still, it was painful for Sarah to surrender a line of study that she had invested so much time and effort to develop.

"Now, before you get all defensive on me, let me tell you something else," said Rhonda in a less strident tone. She was wearing a dark maroon suit with a cream colored blouse. A simple gold chain adorned her once athletic neck. The outfit was very different from the jeans, sneakers and cotton blouses that Sarah wore to work, though her clothes were generally covered by a long, white lab coat. Rhonda leaned back in her chair and tipped her head to the side as she spoke, as if it was a little too heavy from all the CDC experience it contained.

"Riesigoil has promised that they will make this little 'detour' worthwhile for us. According to Oscar, the number on the table right now is in the millions of dollars, and given their history with this institution and the urgency of their request, he felt certain we could count on the money."

Sarah's eyes widened. Oscar was the president of the UT campus in Houston, and if he was involved, that meant that this assignment was even more important than she had originally thought.

"Oh, wow," Sarah said, temporarily at a loss for further words. Securing enough money to sustain research labs like hers, paying for supplies and equipment costs, was a perpetual problem at universities. Copious amounts of researchers' time and energy were used in applying for grants to fund research. For the first time, Sarah found herself warming to the idea.

"Yes, it's a huge deal, Sarah, so humor me for six weeks or so. It could be less. They said they didn't think it would need to be for a longer time period since Megaviridae are a really hot topic and laboratories all over the world are focused on the problem they are having up in the Arctic. It's not in the media yet, but that doesn't mean there aren't a lot of eyes on it."

"Do we know anything about the mode of transmission?"

Rhonda exhaled and reached for a folder on her desk which she slid over to Sarah. "At this time we're not sure how it's transmitted, though it will likely be through aerosols as the people in the field were pretty covered up."

As Sarah flipped through the papers in the folder she ran her left hand through her ponytail. It was something she always did when she was worried or alarmed. Viruses that were transmitted on tiny droplets of moisture in the air, aerosols, were the most difficult ones to prevent from spreading. The common flu and avian flu viruses were also transmitted in this manner. Released from throats or nasal passages, in the form of sneezes and coughs, these viruses could travel quite far.

The highly contagious measles virus could linger in the air for up to two hours after leaving the throat of an infected person, waiting patiently to infect its next victim, as the parents of unvaccinated children who went to amusement parks could attest.

"Ebola and HIV viruses, as you well know," said Rhonda, "are only spread through direct contact of infected bodily fluids with the blood of the recipient. Even tiny cuts on the skin or in the mouth could admit these deadly pathogens, and thus they have spread all too rapidly in vulnerable populations. But this new pathogen seems to begin its infection in the lungs."

Sarah watched Rhonda attentively as she spoke. Her short brown hair was styled attractively around her face, where it remained locked stiffly in place, like castle walls guarding the treasure inside. Heavy black eyeliner wound the circumference of her large dark eyes and her crimson lipstick, which matched her suit, was applied perfectly to her handsome lips, seeming to reflect ruby glints of light as she spoke.

"The Laptev virus has taken out quite a few people up there in one of the research barracks in the Arctic. We need to neutralize it as soon as possible. Finding a cure or a vaccine would be amazing, though I don't expect your team to accomplish something like that in this short of a time frame. However, if we are able to make some decent progress in understanding the biology of Laptev, I can assure you that Riesigoil might be willing to provide resources for four or five years of AIDS research."

Sarah tore her gaze from Rhonda and sought out the dark green leafy branches of the gnarled post oak trees that lined the sidewalks outside the window. Laptev. It was a word that would soon enter the average person's lexicon, just as Ebola and HIV had. She drew in a deep breath and looked around the office. Off to the side were the plaques from Rhonda's degrees and various awards that she had earned while working at the CDC. They were not ostentatious, but they did convey a sense of quiet strength.

"Okay, I understand. We'll take on the Laptev virus project. I just wish it could have waited a few more months."

Rhonda regarded her for a long moment. "I know, Sarah," she said, a bit of compassion leaking into her softening voice. "But even if I wanted to, I couldn't take back the directive to have your team working on the megavirus problem. You see, my hands are tied right now, since Oscar has said that this is a priority."

Then Rhonda smiled conciliatorily and began speaking about the paperwork that would need to be signed. "I'll e-mail you the contract. The company will maintain full ownership of all of the research findings, and you won't be allowed to publish any of the results without full written permission from them."

Sarah reached down to massage her leg, just above the boot, where it throbbed.

"I'll need to inform my team this afternoon," she said, and her tone must have betrayed the doubt and disappointment she felt.

"I know it isn't easy to stop in the middle of a project, Sarah. But it is precisely because your team has experience with strange viruses that you are better suited for this line of investigation than any of the other investigators here at the IDI."

On her way back down to the lab, Sarah thought about the steps that would need to be taken in order to stop their investigations in one area and begin them in another. She needed to have a team meeting and break the news to them. She knew they would be dismayed, but there was no way around it.

After an eternity, the elevator doors whispered open on the third floor and revealed the sign that always made her heart skip just a little bit. MEDICAL MICROBIOLOGY RESEARCH, Sarah Spallanzani, Ph.D. She exited and turned right, heading toward her office.

Sarah's research group consisted of three full-time investigators, Tally, Emile and Drew, and two postdoctoral researchers, Miquela and Shane, as well as several technicians. When they weren't being derailed by Rhonda, former CDC expert, they investigated the human immunodeficiency virus, or HIV, the virus responsible for causing AIDS.

It certainly was a strange virus, Rhonda had that much right. That's why it had taken scientists by surprise when it debuted on the world stage in the late '70s. Sarah pictured her undergraduate virology professor, a passionate man with curly white hair frosting his large head, and who had smoked a pipe during lectures. She remembered when he first introduced the subject of viruses.

"Viruses are relatively simple structures, made up of a strand of genetic information, usually DNA, covered in a protein coat called a capsid. That's it."

Laying his pipe gingerly on a table, he had taken a piece of chalk and drawn a squiggly line on the board to symbolize the DNA, and then a hexagon shape around that to represent the capsid. Then he had wiped his hands together to eliminate the chalk dust, and stepped away, leaving the class to ponder that thought for a few minutes.

Delighted by the simplicity of this definition, Sarah had decided right then and there that she would specialize in virology, not because she believed that viruses were simple structures, but because she was convinced that there was an awful lot behind that simplicity.

Most of Sarah's friends in college were not majoring in science, let alone microbiology, and they tended to use generic terms like "germs," or even worse, "bugs" to describe everything that could induce illness. She had been so exasperated that sometimes she would say in an impassioned voice, "They are not alike at all. Even the simplest bacterium is much larger and more complicated than a virus particle. Bacterial cells have organelles, a circular strand of DNA, cytoplasm, a cell membrane and often a complex cell wall. Furthermore, whereas bacteria and all living cells can be killed, viruses are merely deactivated."

Her friends would roll their eyes and usher her off the soapbox. More disturbing were her first dates that withered when the conversation became intellectual. Discussing science, she had learned, was a great way to make a man lose interest. "Men are intimidated by smart women," her roommate had confided. "If you want dates, you need to play dumb."

But Sarah's indomitable spirit refused to fold neatly into the perfect woman so many of her classmates purported to be. Thus she would return to her dorm after another sour date, gritting her teeth as the bell tower struck nine on a Saturday night.

Graduate school was more fulfilling. She had met her husband and had been briefly tempted to veer from virology by some intriguing cancer research, but had soon returned to her first passion. Now she was surrounded by people who loved to talk about the same things that she did, and she no longer had to apologize for her intelligence. She had endured a post-doctorate in Chicago under a world-renowned virologist, and when the position had opened up at the UT medical school in Houston, she had immediately applied for it.

She loved her work and could often be found discussing the subject of viruses with her graduate students. One of her favorite topics was whether viruses were alive. Sarah felt strongly that anything that could be crystallized was not alive.

"Sugar can be crystallized and turned into rock candy. Sea water could be evaporated to leave only the salt crystals. But nothing that is alive—not even the tiniest cells—can be crystallized and then rehydrated," she would argue. "So if you can crystallize a virus, then it must not be alive."

And yet, there were certainly many people who did not agree. "Viruses, in all their simplicity, are the ultimate parasites," they would say, mysteriously.

"Then what about plasmids?" she would retort, her voice brimming with excitement. She loved discussing cases of infinitesimally smaller structures that were challenging the fragile boundaries of the definition of life all the time.

"They are simple rings of DNA that live inside bacterial cells, but they are separate from bacterial DNA. Their structure is even simpler than that of a virus, and although they can replicate at will, they don't kill their host like viruses do. Plasmids can even pass between different bacterial cells, or different species of bacteria, taking valuable genetic knowledge, such as genes for resistance to antibiotics, with them. Are they alive?"

When new graduate students arrived at her lab, Sarah would quiz them extensively. Many of her students had studied microbiology in their undergraduate careers, but some were biochemists, and she had to be sure that they understood the premises of basic virology before they began working with HIV.

"Tell me how a virus works," she would ask. If the student couldn't answer a basic question like that straight off the bat, she would direct them to go study some more before applying to her lab.

Tally, who had now been working in Sarah's lab for several years, had provided an excellent explanation.

"When a virus gets inside a host cell, such as a bacterium, an amoeba or even a human cell, its DNA takes over the host cell's DNA, becoming the new commander in chief." Sarah had liked that metaphor because it made it clear that the viral DNA was in charge.

"The host cell's DNA, which would normally be directing all cell activity is overthrown, in a coup d'état that is incontrovertible."

Tally had actually used the word *incontrovertible*, just like that. Tally had the most versatile and extensive personal dictionary of anyone who Sarah had ever met, which was saying a lot for someone whose entire life had been in academia. Sarah had suppressed her smile, however, not wanting to make Tally feel self-conscious.

"As in the case of any military takeover, the first thing that the invading viral DNA does is to order the cell to stop what it was doing and instead dedicate itself to making hundreds of copies of the viral DNA and capsids. It is parasitism in its most elemental form. Then, to complete the forced bondage, the host cell is obliged, again under the direction of the viral DNA, to use its own cellular machinery to assemble the viral particles, stuffing each strand of viral DNA into the protein coat and sealing the capsid. In this manner hundreds or even thousands of new virus particles are formed, until the entire cell is filled to bursting with viral particles, and thus perishes, releasing all of the newly formed viruses to attack further cells." Sarah had felt like applauding when Tally had finished with her description. She loved Einstein's quote that if you couldn't explain something simply, you didn't understand it well, and Tally had just proven that she did understand.

"What about HIV?" Sarah asked. It wasn't really a trick question; she just wanted to see how deep Tally's knowledge was before she began her research in earnest. She needn't have worried as Tally answered swimmingly.

"HIV viruses are even more labyrinthine."

Labyrinthine! Another lovely word!

"Instead of DNA, the double-stranded helix molecule which holds the instructions for life in all living organisms, from the simplest bacterium to the most complex mammalian cell, HIV viruses contain RNA, a single-stranded molecule that, upon gaining admittance into a host cell, must first be changed into DNA."

Then she described reverse transcription, and how it had to be accomplished before cellular takeover could begin. "The HIV virus requires an enzyme which does not exist in any living cells: reverse transcriptase." It was a marvelous answer.

Sarah remembered how thrilled and frightened scientists had been in the early 1980s when research on retroviruses was in its pioneer stage. The HIV virus and its kin, whose genetic material had to be changed from RNA to DNA, were fascinating.

Her professor, the same one with the icing hair who had drawn the simple virus on the green chalk board and then walked away, had said, "Not all viruses will immediately attack their host cell, of course, and there are many permutations on the mode of entrance and the exact steps which viruses take to overthrow host cell DNA. Herpes viruses, for example," he said, stopping to take a puff on his pipe, "are quite old viruses, evolutionarily speaking, and thus have evolved to be able to lie dormant within the host cell, say, in the lip of the infected individual, for long stretches of time.

"Herpes viral DNA integrates into the host cell DNA, and when the person makes new cells, the viral DNA is also copied by the human cell machinery, and each daughter cell carries its fresh copies of the virus. That's why once someone has a cold blister, which is really a Herpes infection, it never really goes away. The virus lies dormant until the right trigger, such as a fever or exposure to the sun, frees it from the host cell DNA, awakening the monster which now assumes control of the cell. At that point, the lip cell no longer acts like a lip cell, but instead becomes a Herpes virus factory, creating thousands of copies and then erupting, spilling its contents, new viral particle clones which infect other cells until the body's defense system beats them down. Sacrificed white blood cells and destroyed tissue contribute to creating the pus-filled sore that is the Herpes blister."

It was beautiful and terrifying to think that once you got a cold sore, that viral DNA would be with you, mixing intimately with your own DNA, for the rest of your life. Up until then Sarah had always thought of infections in terms of things your body fought and then they went away. She had not realized that there was literally no way to 'cure' one of a cold sore. The active infection could be tamed, but the virus would be there, lying dormant, always ready to attack.

The HIV virus, instead of infecting lips like the Herpes virus, or nasal and throat passages like the flu viruses, assaults the body's immune system. In particular, the virus infects the specific blood cells responsible for mounting a defense against anything that could invade the body. It is as if a country were attacked, but instead of bombing cities, the invading army only targeted police departments, unequivocally demolishing every one of them. The citizens of the country would be fine for a little while, but with no one able to ever again police the streets, the country would slowly disintegrate from its own petty thievery and picayune acts of crime that would ordinarily have been kept under control.

This is what happened to AIDS victims. Most never perished directly as a result of having the HIV infection, but rather they succumbed to obscure cancers and diseases from which the person's impaired immune system could no longer protect them.

Sarah sat at her office chair and forced herself back to the present. There was a meeting to organize for this afternoon. In the meantime, she would need to begin learning everything she could about dormant viruses emerging from the permafrost.

CHAPTER 5

Sarah's meeting with Rhonda had not been an easy one, and now she had to break the bad news to her team. It wasn't entirely bad news, she told herself as she hobbled toward the elevator. She was trying to put a positive spin on a disappointing situation, but all she could manage was that at least Rhonda trusted them enough to let them handle this new outbreak. She had loads of confidence that no other team could handle this investigation as well as hers could.

Still, having to put aside all of their work and begin a whole new project would be stressful, and she was not pleased at the prospect.

"But, we were making so much progress on AIDS research—why does she want us to turn away now?" asked Tally.

Sarah and her five researchers sat perched on metallic four-legged stools in the teaching lab. They all wore white lab coats, long pants and closed-toed shoes, as safety protocol dictated.

She understood their distress. Research involved a lot of time spent reading and preparing before any experiments were performed, and even more time reading and researching published scientific literature after the results of the experiments came in, no matter what those results were. Experiments had to be repeated multiple times, with every control conceivable in order for the results to be credible.

Sarah recalled when she had first learned about controls. One of her professors had placed three blank sheets of paper, each on black tables in different parts of the room. The students were allowed to walk over to examine each piece of paper, but were not allowed to touch them. Then he asked what color the papers were. The class had immediately replied that they were all white.

"Are you sure?" he asked. Yes, they were sure. Then he had removed the sheet of paper from the first table and placed it partially on top of the second sheet of paper, so that both could be seen, and now the first sheet looked a pale shade of gray when compared to the second sheet. Then he had walked the two pieces of paper to the third table, and sure enough, the last sheet was clearly a different shade, even whiter.

"If I had separated this classroom of people," he said, "and asked each of you to tell me the color of these three items, all of you would have reported that they were white. But only one of them is truly white. When I place it next to the others, that's when I can tell. That's why you need controls in an experiment. Without something to compare your answers against, your answers cannot be trusted."

To further complicate matters, they were working with living organisms and many things could go wrong. How often had cultures become contaminated when instead of being kept warm, they had been allowed to grow cold because the motor on an incubator had gone out? How frustrating was it to accidentally contaminate a bacterial culture when the instruments used to seed it had not been properly sterilized in the high pressure steam autoclave? And if the cells were delicate, like human or mouse culture ones, how exasperating was it to have them explode or shrivel up because the solution in which they were suspended, the buffer, was too salty or not salty enough?

Therefore, Sarah could identify with Tally's frustration at having to change gears and focus on a new set of experiments. "Believe me, I was none too happy about Rhonda's decision either. But she does not have control over this choice. The president of the university is involved in this decision. Apparently the university's focus is off of the AIDS problem for now, since the Laptev epidemic is exploding all over the Arctic."

"Exploding?" asked Emile.

Sarah noticed that Shane, the younger of the two post-docs, made a popping sound with his mouth and moved his fingers as if imitating an explosion. He had only been in her lab for a few months, and Sarah found him to be boorish and quite immature in spite of the fact that he was twenty seven years old. She was still uncertain as to whether he should remain in the lab, but Emile, whom she greatly appreciated as he had worked with her for almost eight years now, had vouched for Shane, saying that he was a hard worker and a clear thinker, even if he occasionally blurted out whatever was on his mind, no matter how inappropriate.

"Okay, poor choice of word, you're right," Sarah conceded.

"Although maybe Sarah has a point. It's killed dozens of people up there," said Drew, thoughtfully. "This is the virus that was discovered under ice, right?"

"Yes, apparently it's one of several gigantic viruses that have been found in the last few years in remote places all over the planet. They discovered another one in the permafrost in Siberia, not too far from where the Laptev one was found, and one down in Chile, under the ocean. This particular virus, the one we'll be investigating, belongs to the group of Megaviridae, which have much larger genomes than the viruses we've always known. I believe some of them are large enough in size to be viewed under a light microscope," said Sarah.

"Whoa! Do you think that the reason more of these viruses are emerging now is because the Arctic is warming at twice the speed of anywhere else on the planet?" said Tally.

"Um," said Sarah. The thought had not crossed her mind.

"I can see the headlines now," said Shane, lowering the pitch of his voice to imitate a newscaster and holding his arm out as if he were placing the words on a giant screen. "'FROZEN VIRUS RELEASED. Scientists say the cold never bothered it anyway.'"

Several people chuckled at the reference to the Disney movie, and Sarah felt some of the tension in the room disperse.

"I remember reading about those megaviruses in one of my graduate virology classes last year, but I thought that they only infected amoebas," said Miquela, bringing the team back to the subject. Miquela spoke softly and clearly, though she always seemed a bit intimidated, often crossing her arms over her chest as she spoke. Sarah thought of her as the more mature of the two post-docs.

She and Shane were about the same age, but Miquela, with her quiet manner and her dark-framed glasses, seemed much more poised and focused on her work.

"That is a question that a good epidemiologist would pose," replied Sarah, beaming at Miquela. "According to Rhonda, the reason researchers thought that it only infected amoebas was because they only provided amoebas as host cells to draw the huge viruses out in the first place. However, the Laptev virus, like several of the other Megaviridae, most likely contains genes for over 2,500 proteins. It is the largest megavirus ever found, and as our bad luck would have it, some of those genes allow it to enter and infect human cells."

"But, what's the mode of transmission? It can't just jump from amoebas into people," said Tally.

"That's one of the questions that researchers haven't quite resolved yet, and one of the first ones we will have to address," Sarah said with a sigh. Rhonda had provided her with a dossier of reports from Riesigoil and in the hours between her meeting with Rhonda and this one with her team, Sarah had skimmed through all of them. Then she had used her university ID to access the world's leading scientific research sites so that she could read up on Megaviridae in general. Most of the scientific information nowadays was inaccessible to the average internet user and required steep subscription prices to even begin searching the sites. Universities spent a lot of money each year to be able to provide access to this information for their researchers.

Sarah's strong foundation in virology, as well as her extensive experience made it easy for her to assimilate a substantial quantity of information in a short period of time and organize it in her mind.

"I heard that the Soviets used to send old submarines full of nuclear waste up to the North Pole and then sink them there, under the ice, and just leave them. Kind of like a dumping ground. Maybe some of them eroded and the radioactive waste had an effect on the virus?" said Shane, squaring his surprisingly broad shoulders for emphasis.

It was a good point. Shane had made so many immature and sometimes annoying comments in the months that he had been working in her lab, that she often didn't pay much attention to him, but this comment showed that he was on-topic and attempting to contribute to the conversation. She did not want to squelch his spirit, and furthermore, she was not certain that his hypothesis was that far-fetched. She had seen the journal articles about the tons of nuclear waste that had been unlawfully disposed of beneath the ice. She looked around at the group, but most were staring either at the ground or at the black stone surface of the lab table, lost in thought.

"Well Shane, at this point we know so little about the problem that I think it's worth it for you to investigate more along those lines," said Sarah. "Obviously you won't be able to immerse yourself in that question, but definitely do check it out and see what you can uncover."

Shane beamed with pride and Sarah thought about how a little thing, a small gesture such as being taken seriously, made such a difference in people's perception of themselves and others. At five foot five, Shane was the shortest male in the lab. He was also one of the youngest in her group, and she imagined that those two facts were probably the reason that he spent so much time trying to stand out in meetings by saying inappropriate things. She would try to remember that he really did have an intelligent mind when she became annoyed with him the next time. Maybe she could regularly find small ways to affirm him to keep him from becoming too crazy with his ideas.

"Also, and probably most importantly, we don't have any idea how to stop Laptev. We don't have a vaccine or any medicines that seem to work," said Sarah. "It will be next to impossible for us to create an effective vaccine in just six weeks, but if we can at least advance in that direction, come up with some clues as to how the next researchers should proceed, it would be important. Let's not lose track of this goal, even if we know we cannot accomplish it."

"The thing is, viruses like Laptev must have been around for thousands of years and no one cared until now," said Emile. He had the slightest of French accents which came across in an ever so soft rounding of words with the letter "r" so that a word like "viruses" sounded more like "*viwuses*."

"They were buried under the ice for thousands of years, not out killing a whole lot of innocent people like they are now," said Drew.

"But really, they haven't killed that many people, in the scheme of things. At least, Laptev hasn't. From what Sarah said, it sounds like a dozen or so, maybe twenty. That's not that many people. No, that's not the reason we care more than we cared about HIV when it first started affecting people." Emile looked around the room, and no one said anything, so he continued. "The real reason we are more concerned now is because this infection is affecting people from first world countries, unlike Ebola. If it were destroying small villages in some remote third world country, we wouldn't even be looking at taking on this project," insisted Emile. "And no one would be asking us to drop AIDS research, when HIV affects so many thousands of people, just to take on this tiny outbreak in the Arctic."

Everyone was quiet for a moment, pondering Emile's words. Sarah knew that he was right, but she also knew that only independently wealthy labs could afford to study whatever they wanted to study. Organizations like theirs, which depended on money from outside sources, did not have that liberty.

"I have a question," said Shane, breaking the thoughtful brooding of the team and raising his hand. "Does the infection look all gross when it gets in people, like Ebola? Does it make their organs dissolve in a pool of blood and their eyes get all bulgy and purple and start to bleed..."

"All right, Shane, I think that's quite enough," said Sarah, cutting him off quickly. She immediately regretted having allowed him to speak in the first place. She should have known that he was going to say something inappropriate when he raised his hand, as if he were still in high school.

"This isn't a Hollywood zombie movie, Shane, it's real life. To answer your question, yes, the physical symptoms are much like those found in Ebola cases, but that's typical of hemorrhagic fever viruses in general. The fatality rate for Laptev is higher than for Ebola though, at 65%, so let me stress again to all of you how imperative it is to go through BSL-4 training again and adhere strictly to the safety precautions at all times when you are working with this virus."

Several people nodded soberly and Sarah decided it was time to wrap up the meeting. "All right folks, we don't have that much time before the transition needs to be complete. Since this new megavirus is so much more contagious than HIV, we have to pack away all of our work and get the lab set up for the new work as quickly as possible. As I just mentioned, safety training will be a priority. Now, I know you all have had that kind of training before, but it's important that you review all of the safety material. I don't want to add any of our names to the list of victims out there. Cool?"

"Have they scrubbed down the labs for the conversion yet?" asked Drew, his long legs stretched out and crossed at the ankles, revealing blue socks under his jeans.

"We've got a crew coming this afternoon. The labs should be ready to go by tomorrow, I believe. It's good that this building is so new."

"When will the first tissue samples arrive?" Tally asked.

"Next Wednesday."

"Wow, that *is* really soon," said Miquela, and then quickly covered her mouth, as if she was embarrassed at having spoken her thought aloud.

"I know," said Sarah. "We've got samples coming in from three different victims. I wish we had more, but they burned the other bodies before anyone thought to sample them."

"And we will be using human tissues for growing the virus?" asked Emile. It sounded like he had said *gwowing the viwus.*

"Actually, I'm thinking we can try two different hosts. We'll use the HeLa line to generate human cells…"

"Gila monster cells? Cool!" said Shane, picking up on the fact that HeLa and Gila had the same pronunciation.

"Not Gila, HeLa, you know, Henrietta Lacks cells?" said Drew.

Shane shook his head. He seemed genuinely puzzled, which made Sarah wonder if his training had been adequate for him to be included in her lab after all. Surely every microbiologist had heard of HeLa cells? They had been around for so many years and had been used so extensively throughout the world.

"It's an immortal cell line that was developed in the 1950s, wasn't it?" said Miquela in a quiet voice.

Shane looked at her, a sneer forming on his face. "Well, there's a gold star for you! So, superman cells to grow the deadly megavirus. Seems fitting, somehow."

Sarah was about to chastise him when she saw Emile catch Shane's eye and shake his head slightly in admonition. To her relief, Shane blushed and looked down.

"Yes, Miquela," said Sarah, as if Shane hadn't spoken. She was determined not to allow him to belittle a fellow female scientist, and anxious that Miquela not feel like she'd done something wrong by knowing more than Shane did. "Poor Ms. Lacks, may she rest in peace, might not have been too happy to know that her cells live on in perpetuity after her cancer took her so suddenly, but her cells have been extremely helpful for scientists around the world as they grow prodigiously quickly. They have been used for all kinds of research which requires human cells. I believe we used some once in our AIDS research as well?"

Tally nodded. "I've got some vials in cold storage. I'll retrieve them and begin cultivating them."

"Excellent," said Sarah. "I'd also like us to take a look at some mouse models."

"Do you think the virus will propagate in mice cells?" asked Miquela. Sarah was pleased that she seemed unscathed by Shane's earlier slight.

"Well, I'm not really sure, but I have a hunch that with so many genes, the Laptev virus might have several different hosts in nature. We don't know what the world looked like when it was frozen in the ice 30,000 years ago, but we do know that there were mammals around, including rodents. What I'm hoping is that passing it through various generations in mice might attenuate the virus enough to be able to handle it better in the lab. We don't want it to change completely, but if it were to become a bit tamer, I don't think that would be a bad thing."

"Yeah, flu viruses are attenuated when we grow them in chicken eggs, so maybe this virus will get weaker in mice. It's a good idea. Certainly worth a try," said Drew.

"It could get worse, though. You never know. Passing it through mice could make it mutate and become 100% fatal," said Shane.

Everyone was silent as they pondered the implications of Shane's words. The truth was that no one knew much at all about the Laptev Hemorrhagic Fever Virus. Soon her lab would be one of a handful of groups who would know more about the virus than anyone else in the world. It was a grim thought.

After the meeting, Sarah shuffled down the hall to the room where the student technicians sat around studying and socializing. Some were undergrads, but several, including Kevin, who looked after the mice that they used for experiments, were graduate students.

"Kevin," she said, addressing the technician who sat at a table in the corner, his books spread out in front of him. There was another young woman sitting at the table with him. Sarah had seen her before—what was her name? Tammy something, she recalled. The girl wore entirely too much makeup, Sarah noted idly, even as she addressed

Kevin. "How are our mice doing? How many do we have?"

Kevin looked up from his cell phone, which he had been poking vigorously. He was one of those people who hardly spoke at all, it seemed to her, preferring instead to live his life online, immersed in whatever social media was most prevalent at the moment. He seldom joined in any meetings, and even when he did, he was never really fully present as the lure of his phone was so strong. In any case, he rarely ever spoke although Sarah strongly suspected that he did nothing in his life without commenting on it electronically.

She had heard Shane telling stories about Kevin's adventures with his smart phone. Apparently it had fallen into the toilet a few months ago. Before that, he had placed it on the hood of his car as he was doing something, then driven off and lost it. Another time he had been texting and walking and he had tripped on the sidewalk. The phone had flown out of his hand and fallen through the grates into the sewer. Sarah figured that he must spend every cent he earned on either buying phones or buying insurance for his phones.

Kevin looked up at her, but did not answer for several seconds. Sarah thought that she would need to repeat her question, but then he said, "Um, I'll speak with the other vivarium techs, but last check, we had quite a few mice to work with."

"Quite a few?" repeated Sarah. She was annoyed with Kevin for not seeming to take her request seriously. Apparently, the line of investigation did not matter much to him. His job was to provide the mice independently of the research topic.

Kevin stared at her blankly for a moment, and then began to scroll through his phone again. She was just about to say something else to him when suddenly he said, "I dunno, but it looks like we have about 200 or thereabouts."

Sarah nodded. "You've got an app for that?"

Kevin looked up at her and grinned his affirmation and suddenly she felt a little fonder of him.

"Good," she said. "I think that's plenty to get the investigations going."

CHAPTER 6

"You look beat, honey," said John. "You coming to bed?"

Sarah sat hunched over her laptop, scrolling through numbers on a spreadsheet. "Yeah, I'll be right there. Give me just a few more minutes to wrap up these notes." Her work was an unapologetically huge part of her life and when a new project got started, it filled her with so much energy that she often found it hard to disengage herself even after she left the lab. Luckily, her husband, also a professor at the university, was equally dedicated. His area of expertise was different, and that meant they often had a lot of things to share with each other.

Sarah finished reading the reports that Riesigoil had sent, jotted down a few quick notes and closed the laptop. Then she stood up and stretched. She was wearing her faded yellow pajamas, the ones with little blue kittens running up the side of the pant legs. Her husband had given her these pajamas when they had first started dating, twelve years ago. They were her favorite ones, not only because they were silky and had lasted so well, but also because of the story that had come with them. John had explained, after they were married, that they had been quite expensive for his grad student's budget, and he had felt both embarrassed and bold as he strode through the aisles of the small shop whose shelves were filled with everything pink, fluffy or lacy. Sarah could easily imagine him blushing as he looked at the endless rows of undergarments and instinctively turned the other way, toward the less intimate apparel.

"I saw all those hangers standing tall with flowing gowns, and little lacy things so I looked around to find a safer shelf, piled high with folded pajamas," he said. The kittens had right away reminded him of Sarah and he had reached for them gratefully, anxious to abort the shopping experiment his best friend had suggested.

Sarah walked over to her husband, who was sitting on the bed holding a journal in his hand, the soft cover folded back and around the pages like a small cylinder. John raised his glasses to his forehead and smiled at her. "Tea?"

"Yes, please," she said, and almost felt like purring when he reached out and began massaging her shoulders.

Then, by adjusting the pressure on her shoulders, he turned her around to face him. Sarah loved the way he looked at her, always apparently pleased by the sight. It made her feel attractive. Luxuriating in his admiring stare, she pulled her hair loose from the ponytail she always wore, and shook her hair out. It was dark and curly, and hung quite far down her back.

John winked at her as he rose from the bed and headed toward the kitchen of their small apartment. Sarah followed him there, though more slowly. Her leg was always more painful at night.

"This Laptev Virus project is going to be a real challenge. We've been working on the AIDS project for so long and we'll have to shake things up a bit to change gears."

"It does suck, but you always love a new challenge," he said, his eyes twinkling. "Weren't you getting bored with that other virus?"

"*Bored?* John, we were finally starting to make real progress."

"Seems to me that that's the perfect time to begin doing something else."

Sarah made a *hrmph* sound and rolled her eyes. She knew that her husband was teasing her. "Well, I just hope Rhonda's confidence in my team is well-placed and that we can figure something out, you know. Six weeks is such a short window of time. It's almost laughable. You can barely begin to sink into a simple research problem in six weeks, let alone find answers to what's killing those people up there in the Arctic and how to stop it. It's going to be a tough nut to try to crack."

"Is your whole team going to be working with you?" he asked, handing her an oatmeal raisin cookie.

Sarah sighed and took a bite, then held it out, inspecting it. She was always interested in how many raisins had made it into her cookie. The poor ones averaged less than five raisins, and the really good ones had more than ten, guaranteeing several in each bite. Hers had eight. She chewed slowly and then said, "Yeah, though that's another bone of contention. They were none too happy about the change in projects, you know. But, they won't be that way for very long. We'll get the lab all ready to go and get the new tissue samples and everyone will be off and running."

"Everyone except you, sweetheart," said John, motioning to her propped leg.

Sarah smiled. "Yeah, sheeze, I'm ready for it to stop hurting so much."

She watched as he poured the steaming tea into matching cups, added honey to his, and milk to both, then carefully stirred.

"Well, I think it's a compliment," he said, now reaching over and touching Sarah's face softly. She felt herself relaxing again with his touch and the tightness she had felt all afternoon began dissolving.

"She has a lot of confidence in you," he continued, "rightly so, if I do say so myself. And, this is a great opportunity for your team to be able to help and make a difference. Besides, six weeks isn't that long, like you said, so you'll be back to your AIDS research before the end of the summer."

Sarah exhaled disheartenedly. "You're right, I know you are. And I said these same things to myself this afternoon. But still, I was feeling bad about it just now, as I thought about it some more."

John nodded. "Did I tell you about the studies we've just started?" he asked.

Sarah shook her head. Her husband worked in the Neuropsychology Department where he led a team that investigated personality disorders. Over the last several years his team had been focusing on fear, attempting to elucidate the specific chemicals that were released in the brain when that emotion was present, and analyzing how those chemicals were metabolized. How could they be adequately managed? Why were some brains more prone to releasing those chemicals, and thus more likely to be fearful, than others? His team also investigated teenage brains, since this age group seemed to not act out of fear.

Thus they were asking what went on in adolescent brains as compared to what occurred in adult brains—did they release fewer fear chemicals, which in turn made them more likely to try something more daring, or did they process the chemicals quicker, thus diminishing their effect on the brain?

"We've just started working with mouse models. We've partnered with a group from Stanford, and we'll be doing research with specific known triggers. I'm pretty excited about it," John said, and then, as they sat and sipped their tea, he told her about his new research plans. Instead of the typical scenarios involving mazes and man-made challenges, they would be using triggers that were hard-wired in mice.

"You mean like cats?" Sarah asked.

"Absolutely! My colleague at Stanford has been working with mouse behavior to elucidate what part of the cat induces the fear response. Is it the smell of the cat's body, the smell of its urine, the sound of its claws on the ground, the look of its fur, its speed, the sound of its meow or hiss, the look of its open mouth, teeth or its eyes—what is it about the cat that induces the most fear in mice?"

"Surely it's the whole cat, I would think," said Sarah.

"Maybe, maybe not. For some animals it's the shape of the body of their predator that induces fear. People who are afraid of snakes, for example, will register systemic reactions to a two dimensional shape of the shadow of a snake. And gorillas are frightened of toy crocodiles."

"No way! Gorillas are smarter than that, aren't they?" shot back Sarah, playfully. She loved challenging her husband this way.

"They are quite clever, true, but at least some of them are afraid of toy crocodiles. Let me tell you a story: I once read about a neat set of experiments about a gorilla who was taught sign language. The trainer had an area where she didn't want the gorilla to go, and she found that simply telling the gorilla not to go there didn't stop him from doing so. He understood perfectly, but he did it anyway. So she put a toy crocodile there, and the gorilla immediately stopped going to that area."

"Really? Couldn't it tell that the crocodile wasn't real?"

"Yes, I believe so, but it said that it was still afraid."

"It *said*?"

"With sign language."

"Oh, right."

"Which means that you can't just assume things about triggers that induce fear. Like you, with spiders."

Sarah shivered. "I hate them."

"See, just mentioning the word gets a reaction from you. And now if I draw this," said John, quickly sketching a frightening image of a spider. He showed it to his wife and she grimaced.

"You see? Intellectually you know it's only an image, just paper with ink, but it still evokes a visceral feeling from you. So it could be that the shape of a cat will do so to mice as well."

"But, that can't possibly be ingrained, John. If the mouse has never seen a cat, it might not know to fear it. I mean, you always hear stories about unlikely pairs of animals becoming friends. Ducks following a dog around, a pig and sheep being friends, things like that."

John took a sip of tea, considering. "That's true. Well, we shall see what happens. But the point of this whole story of mine is that you aren't the only one starting on something new. We'll both have lots of new things to think about over the coming weeks."

Sarah nodded and smiled. John always made her feel better, no matter what.

CHAPTER 7

"So, where are we in terms of transmission?" asked Sarah. Since beginning research on the Laptev virus, she had become much more involved in the ongoing work of her researchers, and she was holding weekly meetings with them. Before, when they were investigating AIDS, she used to only meet with them about every two weeks, unless someone needed a more frequent reunion. This gave her more time, in turn, to focus on filling out grant applications and securing the necessary money to be able to purchase the expensive materials and supplies that they used, as well as to cover the salaries of her researchers. Writing the essays that grant forms required was practically a full-time job, and one which Sarah did not enjoy at all, but it was a reality in almost every university setting across the world.

"We've been able to confirm that it's definitely a virus that is contained in the ice and that can be transmitted through the air," said Drew. "We tried an experiment with an untainted sample of ice core that the company sent us. In an air-tight chamber, we placed human cells in open containers near the top walls of the hood, and used a hammer to smash the bits and release a few particles into the air. Within a few hours, the cells begin showing signs of infection."

Sarah pictured the tissue culture hood, also called a laminar flow cabinet, in her mind. It was like a stainless steel box, often about three feet wide and two feet deep and perhaps 3 feet tall. Hoods were always incorporated onto a table or cabinet so that the base of the chamber was waist height and could be easily used when standing. The front of the chamber was covered with a sliding glass door. When the door was raised open, it disappeared into a slot at the top of the hood. Powerful and precisely aimed fans sent a strong layer of air down the front of the hood, where the glass door had been, creating an invisible curtain-like barrier across which the air in the room could not casually cross on tiny currents. This air curtain, known as laminar flow, also helped to protect the workers as airborne microbes tended to be trapped inside the hood when scientists were working with their arms reaching into the hood, while the rest of their body remained outside.

The inner "ceiling" of the chamber was a huge extraction vent, like the ones over a kitchen stove, but much more potent. Drew and his colleagues had probably used metallic clamps to hold the cells, growing on the inside part of transparent plates, to expose them to the bits of flying ice.

"Good work," said Sarah, "but it's bad news. That makes this virus the most dangerous one we have ever worked with. We all need to proceed with utmost caution. Aerosol viruses are really difficult to stop. Has everyone in the lab undergone the training for working with these viruses again?"

Sarah looked around and saw everyone assenting.

"I really don't want to lose anyone," she said seriously. "I cannot overstate the danger here. If you are the least bit tired or stressed, I don't want you doing any experiments with Laptev, until you feel better, is that clear? I know we are under a time crunch, trying to find some answers in just a matter of weeks, but let me remind everyone that stress can lead to sloppy technique, and that could be harmful or fatal, so no one is going near the BSL-4 rooms if you are not fully focused on your work."

Sarah felt a little like one of her professors who used to beat them up about the obvious things, but she preferred to err on the side of oversimplification than to assume that everyone understood the dangers and then later find out that someone had made a simple error in judgment and become contaminated with Laptev.

"All right, what else have we got?" Sarah asked. She looked fondly at her group of researchers with their lab coats buttoned to varying degrees. Emile, who was by far the neatest of them, always had an immaculate coat with his name embroidered on the pocket over his left breast. Shane, who was at the other end of the spectrum, had a stained coat, with one of the lower pockets partially ripped, its corner flapping uselessly. Where most everyone had their first and last names on their coat, Shane had only his first name messily scrawled in permanent ink over the breast pocket, as if it were an afterthought.

"I did some sleuthing into a plausible theory for its origin," said Tally, reaching back to tighten her short ponytail. Her hair was barely long enough to pull back so she had to readjust it frequently.

Sarah smiled. She knew that Tally must have done this work outside of her time spent in the lab as Tally had been quite immersed in hands-on work with the HeLa cells, getting them ready for use as hosts, and this task had occupied countless hours in the lab. "Great, what did you come up with?"

"Well, what tipped me off was when you told us the part about the workers dropping the ice core sample."

"Ha!" said Shane, "that's a no-brainer. I would have dropped it too if bears had shown up!"

"Shane," said Sarah.

"I was just saying," he said, smirking and shrugging his shoulders.

"I was thinking about how the virus could have infected the men," said Tally. "It's an entirely different situation from when the AIDS virus debuted in Africa. Of course, HIV is transmitted from body fluids of infected hosts, and Ebola is the same, but with this virus, there were no infected fluids. Plus, it's really cold there, so people were covered up, for the most part, so I wondered about transmission. I did some reading about the weather conditions up there in Laptev Bay, and it was clear that the workers would have been fully suited up in clothing to protect them from the weather, including gloves, though in the summer it doesn't look like facial gear is used."

Sarah nodded. She too had recognized that the fact that the ice core sample had been dropped and broken had probably played a role in transmitting the virus.

"Also, I was thinking about the lab technicians who got infected after the outdoor crew had been exposed. Both sets of men contracted the viral infection within hours of each other. Therefore it could *not* have been the ones who retrieved the ice core sample who were responsible for infecting the lab techs. It was too short a time frame for the outdoor workers to have developed a high enough titer of virus in their systems to become infectious."

"That makes sense," said Shane, scratching his chin. "In just a couple of hours those outdoor workers would not have been sick enough to be sneezing the virus to someone else yet."

"Exactly. So the lab techs had to have become ill from the direct source of the virus. I read up about standard procedure for analyzing ice core samples, and I realized that the lab techs had probably always worked with prior ice cores in a completely protected environment because they wanted to be able to calculate the amount of gases trapped in the air bubbles, and if the sample was exposed to air, that data would have been invalid."

"So, you were thinking that Laptev could possibly have been a danger before, if it was present in other ice core samples, but it was one that no one realized because when they followed standard protocol, no one was ever exposed and consequently, no one got sick," said Emile.

Sarah noticed out of the corner of her eye that Miquela was nodding, enthralled in the conversation. Shane, however, looked bored, and Kevin, who had decided to sit in on the meeting, was, as usual, keeping quiet but tapping away on his phone.

Tally nodded enthusiastically, her short dark blonde hair, loose again from the tie, was bobbing as she spoke. "Precisely. And so I was thinking about what was *different* this time. Why were they more exposed? It occurs to me that since the lab techs knew that the sample had been dropped and cracked open, they were no longer looking for data that could only be extracted from intact, uncontaminated samples. So they probably didn't take the normal precautions such as placing the samples in a sterile and enclosed environment as they had always done before.

They would still have proceeded in a climate controlled environment, to keep the ice from melting too quickly, and worked with it under aseptic conditions, but they would not have necessarily worn protective masks, not supposing that anything virulent could be present."

"Agreed," said Sarah. "I bet you're right."

"They live in close quarters and it's always cold, so when people began getting sick, it would not have initially have been a cause for alarm."

"Until the symptoms of hemorrhagic fever emerged and everyone started bleeding all over the place," said Shane. Sarah was surprised for she had thought that he was not paying attention at all, but he obviously was.

"...by which time it was too late to take effective isolation and quarantine measures. That's why everyone, or nearly everyone, was exposed in a pretty short time span," concluded Tally.

"Riesigoil's quick response certainly helped to save lives. If only the storm hadn't hit and they could have evacuated the crew even quicker," said Drew.

Everyone was silent as they contemplated that thought.

"Got anything else?" asked Sarah, flexing her knee slightly as her sore leg was getting stiff.

"Yeah, here's one more thing that I found interesting. What I was wondering is how did this virus get there in the first place? I mean, how did it get into the ice in Laptev Bay? Since not all viruses affect all animals, I figured that those poor workers who became ill were probably not the first humans to come in contact with the virus," said Tally.

Sarah remembered the first time she learned about virus specificity. Although there were a few viruses, like some flu viruses, which could go from one species to another, most viruses could not. It had to do with how they attached to the cells in the first place in order to enter them. Cells of different species had differently shaped membranes. For that matter, cells within each body tissue had differently shaped membranes. This meant that someone could sneeze on your toes as much as they wanted to, and you would not get sick unless you breathed in the air that had those flu viruses. It also meant that Tally was right and that in all likelihood, the Laptev virus had seen humans before or otherwise it would not be making anyone sick now.

"Go on," said Sarah. She was quite impressed that Tally had followed up on her musings and found out some facts to begin to shed some light on the situation.

"It turns out that humans have lived on the shores of Laptev Bay for time immemorial. So then I began wondering how long 'time immemorial' could be. We know that ancient humans were itinerant, and that they migrated over the Bering Straits some 15,000 years ago, in pursuit of mammoths, right? That's how they crossed over from Asia to America. But, if they were successful 15,000 years ago, how long before *that* did they attempt to find a passage and not succeed? And where all did they wander before they actually found the Bering Straits?"

Sarah had to smile. "You think like a detective, Tally. I love it!" she said, laughing. Despite her initial misgivings about the project, Sarah realized that it felt really good to be so focused on this interesting question and to see how well her research team was evolving. She was certain that this was a special team, and that another combination of investigators might not have made nearly as much progress in such a short period of time.

Tally sat up straighter and smiled as she continued telling her story. "We don't have written records that go that far back in time, of course, and there aren't any caves around there where we could find traces of ancient human activity. So I had to think of a different way to answer that question. Then I remembered that a while ago I read an article in National Geographic about how there are people who are hunting mammoth tusks. So I went back and looked for the article because I was pretty sure they were talking about somewhere way up north."

Sarah felt a thrill of excitement at Tally's words and she could see that everyone else was also completely focused on her story. Even Kevin had stopped poking at his phone.

"It turns out that it is in the frozen tundra of Siberia where they are looking for the tusks. Apparently these fossil ivory tusks appear all over the place up there because the cold has helped to preserve them, and the mammoths must have been everywhere."

Sarah felt another tingle of excitement and immediately began to anticipate where Tally's story was going.

"Then I did more research on our university data base about mammoth ivory, and sure enough, I saw that some tusks had been found on the shores of Laptev Bay."

Emile let out a short whistle of surprise, and Miquela raised her hand to her mouth. Everyone was astounded by Tally's discovery.

"So, although it's certainly not been proven beyond a doubt, I'm willing to bet that there were humans in the area of Laptev Bay 30,000 years ago, chasing those mammoths around. They must have caught the virus back then and perished, but some of the virus particles remained trapped in the ice and lay hidden there until we pulled them out of their icy grave, all these thousands of years later."

Sarah beamed with pride. "Tally, that is an amazing story. Bravo! It sounds to me like the makings of a *Science* or *Nature* article. I think you'd better start putting something together." She imagined what it would be like to have an article published in either of those top journals of the scientific world. It would be a dream come true. Most investigators, she knew, never got a chance to come across something so interesting that it could be considered for publication in one of those journals, and here they were, after only two weeks of working with Laptev, already contemplating sharing their results with the world in such a dramatic fashion.

And why shouldn't they? In spite of efforts to suppress them, reports about the incidents involving the trapped Arctic workers and the spanking new hemorrhagic flu virus had swiftly leapt across the social media platforms. 'Laptevgate' had captivated the attention of millions who listened to the same news over and over, like desperate gamblers hoping that the next nickel will cause the slot machine to spew out its rich bowels.

Headlines from several local and national newspapers read, "Perilous Polar Pathogen Persists after 30,000 Years" and "Arctic Contagion Kills 7" and "Glacial Outbreak Closes Barracks; Workers Flown Home."

"That reminds me," said Drew, reaching for a newspaper that was lying folded open on the table. "I wanted to read you all this article from today's *Chronicle*. Its title is 'Houston, We Have a Problem.' Listen to this:

> Scientists at the University of Texas Medical School are rushing to investigate the slew of deaths caused by a hitherto unknown pathogen, the alleged LAPTEV HFV, discovered by accident when Riesigoil workers were taking

routine ice core samples. 'It was a very regrettable loss of life,' said Riesigoil CEO, Stan Sundback, who is no stranger to misfortune. A former executive at BP, Sundback was one of the senior managers overseeing the Deepwater Horizon venture in the Gulf of Mexico when the explosion took place in March, 2010, killing 11 workers and injuring 16 others.

'We were very fortunate to secure the help of the UT researchers,' said Sundback. He was referring to the investigative group under the direction of the Head of Infectious Disease Investigation Department, Dr. Rhonda Bentley, former director of the Center for Disease Control. 'I've got an excellent team focused like a high power laser on this problem,' said Bentley in a phone interview.

Meanwhile, citizens in Houston are taking precautions. 'I'm staying indoors and cranking up the AC,' said Kenneth McClintock, owner of a local brewery. 'It's July in Houston anyways, so I'm telling all of my customers to come on in and have a cool drink. That a-ways they can escape from the heat and the mosquitoes. We all know those nasty bugs can carry all kinds of viruses like West Nile virus and maybe even Ebola. Who knows if Laptev VHF can be transmitted that way too? It certainly might could, says I, and I, for one, am not gonna take any chances.'

Donald Carson, Head of the Mosquito Control Division of the Harris County Public Health and Environmental Services, seemed to agree with McClintock. 'In light of a possible virus epidemic, Harris County legislators have issued an emergency decree to increase surveillance of mosquito populations and analyze samples, especially near schools and hospitals. We are also considering what steps should be taken to control mosquito populations which could be implicated in the spread of Laptev HFV. It's not too early to take precautions.'

Sarah did not know whether to laugh or cry when Drew finished reading. She was a bit annoyed that she and her team had not been mentioned by name, but then again, the message in the article had been so flawed that it was probably a good thing not to have her name in there.

"Did he really say 'Laptev *VHF*'? Seriously? Is he thinking it's some sort of old video or do you think it was a typo?" asked Emile.

"He also said 'that a-ways' and 'might could' so I bet it wasn't a mistake," said Shane, chuckling.

Sarah smiled. She remembered how surprised she had been to hear educated people, even TV news anchors saying 'might could' and 'might should' when she had first moved to Texas. Some of her friends from Louisiana also spoke that way.

"And mosquitoes as vectors, indeed. Where did *that* idea come from?" said Tally, shaking her head.

"You should see how many hits there are on #Laptev, #Megavirus and #Arcticfever on Twitter," said Kevin.

"It's true," said Shane. "Last night I saw a Facebook group to support Laptev Bay survivors and their family members."

"My mom said she found Pinterest pictures of black and white electron microscope photographs and drawings of megaviruses. She asked me if I knew what they could be," said Tally.

"And every news talk show host is discussing the 'megavirus problem'. Did you guys see Steven Colbert on the *Late Show* a few nights ago?" asked Emile. He made *Colbert* sound undeniably French when he said it.

"Oh, I saw that," said Tally. "He was awesome. He said something like 'Isn't it ironic that oil drilling in the Arctic actually *is* as bad for the world as the environmentalists and Green Peace volunteers have predicted all along that it would be?' It was great."

CHAPTER 8

A week after Sarah's meeting with her team, Angela sat at her desk reviewing reports which had come in from other parts of the Arctic. As Vice President of Health, Safety and Environment at Riesigoil, she had access to the files on all of the incidents that had occurred in the company's history, and she also could access safety incident reports that had been made on behalf of other companies. She was checking carefully to be sure she hadn't missed any other cases of flu-like illnesses that might have occurred anywhere in the vicinity of Laptev Bay over the last few years. If there were any other incidents, she knew, journalists would have a field day, alleging that the irresponsibility shown by the big bad oil companies was never to be underestimated.

When she finished going through all of the files, she gave a sigh of relief. No other American companies had filed reports of incidents in the past ten years, although there did seem to be an inordinate number of worrisome rumors of flu-like incidents among workers in the Russian companies. But it was impossible to tell. The reports from those companies were not available to her. Good ol' Putin and his secrecy.

"Dr. Redi, there's a call for you on line one. It's Mr. Sundback."

Angela thanked her assistant.

"Hi, Stan, how are you?" she said smoothly to her boss.

She had a good relationship with him and she admired the sensitivity and kindness with which he treated her and all of the employees. When he first hired her a year ago, he told her that he was proud that Riesigoil had fewer injuries and fatalities than any other oil and gas company of similar size, and he made sure that she understood that he would always follow through on any recommendation that her office deemed important.

"I had a really bad experience when I was in your shoes at another company, you see," he said.

She saw grim lines of sadness around his mouth and eyes as he spoke.

"You worked as a VP of Safety as well?" she asked, suddenly seeing him in a new light. Many CEO's were just business people who often didn't know that much about the industry they were running. Sure, they learned, but they weren't necessarily promoted from within the system.

"I did. At British Petroleum, or Beyond Petroleum, as they call it now. Unfortunately, my superiors were not at all interested in what I had to say."

Then he told her about the worst experience he had had. He had presented multiple reports to his boss with serious concerns about numerous incidents the Deepwater Horizon had incurred prior to the explosion, but they had largely been ignored.

"We were five weeks behind schedule because so many things had gone wrong already. Did you know that in 2008 the entire platform tilted to one side and began to sink and we had to evacuate 77 people?"

Angela had read the extensive reports on the findings of the disaster, but she listened quietly to his story.

"And many of the engineers had concerns even a year before the explosion because of the quality of the metal casing that they wanted to use for the well. They said it could collapse under high pressure and I dutifully pointed this out, but my reports were pushed aside. And as a result people died and were seriously injured. BP, of course, sued Transocean and a few other companies, to deflect blame."

"And what happened to you, if I may be so bold?"

"I was 'advised' to leave shortly after the disaster. It allowed BP to show that they were taking 'serious action to address the terrible disaster.' I didn't mind though. I couldn't continue working for a company like that," said Stan, shaking his head. "Then Riesigoil hired me and it's been a great company to work for."

Angela had felt confident about taking the position after this conversation. Now, as she sat in her own office listening to Stan, she pressed the phone more tightly against her ear as she focused on Stan's words.

"I gotta tell ya," he said, diving to the heart of the matter as he always did. "The shareholders are putting a lot of pressure on us. I had a long talk with Dennis Perey, the Chairman. He said that they want results soon or they'll be pulling out and selling their stock. If several of the big ones sell, Angela, it will be bad. Riesigoil could tank pretty quickly."

Angela clenched her teeth in frustration as she gripped the phone tightly. "But surely they understand that we can't send people back up there to drill until we know more about the virus? It's not just Riesigoil—any company would protect its workers. Can't they see that?"

She remembered how distraught he had been when the Arctic incident had occurred in early May. He told her that he had hardly been able to sleep as the reports of the calamity had arrived. And he had quickly authorized the closing down of the barracks, against the wishes of the board, as well as generous funding for immediate research into the nature of the virus.

"I know," said Stan, letting his breath blow through his lips noisily. "But it seems that the situation has gotten more complicated in the past few weeks. Apparently Glassuroil, the other company that has land holdings close to ours, has declared that it will be drilling in the Arctic starting next week. They finished all of the initial investigations that we were still working on. Then they went on to complete an exploratory well in record time and now Glassuroil plans to sink a permanent well. So the shareholders are afraid that they will tap into a big reservoir before Riesigoil does. I tried to explain to them about the quarantine, but the shareholders are having none of it."

Angela fidgeted in her chair and began running her finger over the edge of her desk. It was a nervous habit. "Stan, I know I don't need to remind you that *seven* people perished up there. Seven out of a group of fifteen. Three others are still in intensive care, though, thankfully, it looks like they will pull through. But it's abundantly clear that we shouldn't send any workers back to that area before we get a better handle on what's going on. I mean, what if drilling begins and more people get sick? I just don't see how we could do that."

"You're preaching to the choir here, Angela. I totally hear you. The problem is that there is an awful lot of money invested in this venture. A staggering amount of money. And time's a wastin'. If we don't get at least a few more exploratory wells dug before September, we'll lose another nine months as the winter sets in and closes up the Arctic till next year."

"Winter will close the Arctic for everyone, though, right?"

Stan didn't respond.

"Stan, what is it? Will Glassuroil..." she left the question open.

She could hear Stan tapping his pencil against the desk. Tap, tap, tap, tap, tap.

"Dennis says that they have learned that if Glassuroil gets a good well going, they'll keep their people up there till December, maybe even later. They've signed a deal with Moscow and so they've got huge icebreaker ships already lined up. The Arctic is taking longer to freeze each winter lately, and thawing quicker, and that means that those nine months are becoming more tenuous. No one would want to go up there for the first time, in, say, late September or October, but an established group based in Siberia would have no reason to rush home. Anyway, according to our intelligence reports Glassuroil just issued an internal statement to that effect last night, so our shareholders are getting jittery.

Intelligence reports. Angela smiled in spite of herself. When she had first learned that oil companies had extensive spy networks set up, she had been quite surprised. But the necessity of these operatives had become obvious over the year that she had worked at

Riesigoil, and she knew that larger companies went as far as contracting former CIA and FBI undercover agents to investigate all sorts of matters related to their competition. Big money elevated the stakes.

"And if a large enough group of shareholders were to get trigger happy and pull the plug..."

"There would go Riesigoil," said Angela, completing his sentence. She heard Stan's pencil tapping once again they both contemplated the implications.

"Along with our jobs and the jobs of many, many people. We'd sink quicker than Enron did."

"I get it," said Angela, letting out a deep sigh. "Look, let me check with Oscar at the University. I'll see if they've been able to shed more light on the matter. If I can find any way around our situation, any way at all to get those barracks opened again in the next couple of weeks..."

"I knew you'd understand, Angela. I mean, I certainly don't want to lose any more people to the virus either, but maybe they can figure something out—just enough for us to be able to get back up there and work around it, you know?"

She did know. He had already demonstrated that the safety of all of the employees in his company was paramount to him and she trusted that he would not put any lives at risk unnecessarily. He wanted results, of course, otherwise he would be a lousy CEO, but not at the expense of the safety of the workers.

"How soon do you think you can get an answer from Oscar?"

"I'm not sure, Stan, but I'll convey the urgency of the matter and let you know as soon as I have any news."

After she hung up, Angela sat thinking about what Stan had said. She had known that the situation was bad and that Riesigoil needed the issue resolved as soon as possible, but she had not imagined that the company would flounder and drown if the competition got to the oil first. Surely there were other opportunities? Weren't they involved in fracking operations to harvest natural gas in west Texas?

She wished that she could speak to the shareholders directly and explain the situation, maybe show them some pictures of what had happened. But after another few moments she realized that if she could have direct contact with them, her news might have the opposite effect, and rather than convince them to be patient, it would push them over the edge, making it easier for them to pull their money out quickly and leave the company to hemorrhage, just as the Laptev virus had done to its victims.

No, it was better that Stan worked with the shareholders. He knew how to deal with them more than she knew or cared to know. She would handle this end much better. For now, the most pressing need was for further information. She tapped her cell phone and began scrolling through her contacts to find Oscar Mitchell's number, but when she found it, she paused. It was entirely too easy to evade questions by phone, and she could not afford to have him postpone their conversation. She needed to understand the progress first-hand, preferably today. After all, it had been three weeks since her last meeting with Oscar. That should have been plenty of time for him to have come up with at least a few answers.

Angela notified her assistant to cancel the rest of her meetings for the afternoon. It was only a twenty minute drive from her office in the Energy Corridor to the UT Medical School building in Houston's museum district. She called Oscar and informed him that she would be paying him a visit in person to discuss the progress that was being made. For some meetings, she knew, there was no better way to apply pressure than to show up in person, holding the purse strings tightly in one's hand. If the university wanted to receive further funding from Riesigoil, they would have to start providing some interesting information soon.

CHAPTER 9

Three weeks had passed since Sarah and her team had been asked to drop their research on AIDS and focus on Laptev instead. Although her lab was not that large, there were times when the investigators immersed themselves so thoroughly in their experiments that there was not much interaction between the individuals. Sarah liked it when there were fewer meetings as it gave people a chance to really focus, without being asked to report their progress every two seconds. Her investigators seemed to feel the same way. However, every one of her investigators had apparently made tremendous progress and had much to report.

It was Thursday afternoon and their weekly meeting was already in progress when there was a knock on the door of the lab. Sarah looked through the glass panels that framed the door and saw Rhonda, accompanied by Oscar Mitchell, the University President and another woman. Oscar was easily recognizable with his bushy eyebrows that ran together, but who was the woman with him? Certainly not anyone from another lab—she was dressed too nicely, in a classy dark gray pants suit and open-toed pumps. A mixture of dread and irritation washed over Sarah.

"Whoa, look who's come to visit. Somebody must have screwed up royally," said Shane under his breath.

"Tone it down," hissed Emile.

"Sorry, I was just sayin'. It's not every day that royalty come to visit," said Shane, far from contrite.

Sarah ignored their comments and rose to answer the door. She was busy trying not to think that Rhonda was throwing her under the bus, popping into her meeting unannounced and with visitors. How difficult was it to be a bit more considerate of your colleagues?

"Sorry to barge in on you like this," said Rhonda. Sarah saw that Rhonda held her gaze a bit longer than was necessary and then she darted her eyes to the side. Suddenly the coin dropped and Sarah understood—it was not Rhonda's idea to crash the meeting like this. Something urgent must have happened. Her apprehension remained, but some of her annoyance vanished.

"I've got two distinguished visitors with me this afternoon," continued Rhonda, her voice a slightly higher pitch than usual. "You remember Oscar Mitchell, our university president?"

Sarah accepted his extended hand and kept her eyes from flitting to his eyebrows.

"And this is Angela Redi, Vice President of Safety and Health…"

"Health, Safety and Environment at Riesigoil," said Angela, extending her hand in turn to Sarah.

Riesigoil. Sarah smiled and shook hands even as she felt her stomach sinking. Riesigoil. Wasn't that the name of the company which had had the Laptev virus incidents? Of course! And that meant that they were funding her research now, through a sizable donation. Rhonda had only mentioned the company's name once, and Sarah had barely noted it, being much more concerned with the science than the politics. Now she chided herself for not having looked up the company. The name had sounded foreign and she assumed that it was located somewhere in another country. But here was their HSE VP, speaking in perfect English, and not at all looking like she'd just hurried off a plane and raced through Customs and come straight to the university.

They exchanged pleasantries, and Rhonda made sure to drop the word 'Laptev virus'. She was trying to help make things clear for Sarah in a subtle manner, in case she had not yet understood. Then Rhonda asked if it would be all right if they sat in on the meeting. Sarah froze for only an instant, then recovered and forced herself to smile. She graciously ushered her illustrious guests into the lab. Since they usually just sat around on lab stools, Sarah experienced a moment of panic, thinking it might be better to move the meeting to the conference room where everyone could sit in a proper chair, but her visitors immediately rejected that idea.

"Well then, your timing is impeccable," said Sarah, struggling to regain her composure. "We only just got started a few minutes ago with our weekly progress meeting. Let me present my team to you."

Once lab stools had been found for the visitors, Sarah introduced her investigators and asked them to say a few words about themselves and their role in the Laptev virus project. Then Sarah recapped last week's meeting briefly, explaining Tally's working hypothesis about humans living in the Laptev Bay area all those thousands of years ago as they followed the mammoths around, and perhaps succumbing to the virus in that location.

Then, crossing her fingers that her team would respond well, she motioned to Tally and Drew, and said, "All right, let's get going here. Would you mind starting over and telling us all what you two found out about the ice core sample analysis this past week? I believe you had some more specific information about how the virus suddenly became virulent again after lying dormant for 30,000 years?" It was as good a place as any to begin, and she felt fairly confident Tally and Drew would respond well.

"Okay," said Drew, taking the lead in the presentation they had planned. "Our first question, following up from our presentation last week was regarding whether the appearance of the Laptev virus at the site where they took the ice core sample was an isolated incident or whether the virus was present in other locations nearby."

At this point Angela nodded and Sarah guessed that she must have also wondered about that question.

"We were able to get an audience with a geologist from Riesigoil," said Drew, glancing quickly toward Angela.

Sarah's eyes widened slightly as she realized that this meant that her researchers had paid more attention than she had to the company who was sponsoring their investigations. Well, she thought, good thing they weren't oblivious like me.

"He's a guy named Russ Morrison," continued Tally, taking up the story, "and he was assigned to the Laptev Bay drilling area. He turned out to be instrumental and had some interesting things to tell us. First off, in regards to that ice core sample taken on the day the bears attacked: it turns out that part of the reason it slipped out of the bore and broke so easily was because the ice was already softening. Russ said that they had done some geological sound wave analyses earlier in the week in that area, and they found that the ice shelf above the area where they were expecting to hit land and drill for oil had been melting, and apparently it was melting at a faster rate than they had expected. I don't think that the research team that was sent out to get the ice core sample that day was aware of that, or otherwise they would have perhaps taken extra precautions in handling it."

"Like making sure no bears were around?" asked Shane ironically.

Sarah felt mortified and noticed that Angela blanched.

"Perhaps," said Tally, clearly not taking the bait. "But there's another thing which no one mentioned earlier, that Russ thought might be important, and that is the fact that they had already drilled exploratory wells only a kilometer away."

Angela nodded, but made no comment. Sarah realized that she, too, must have also known this.

"Now why is this important to us?" asked Drew, rhetorically. "It's important because if the Laptev virus was also present in those samples, it would mean that its prevalence is more widespread and that it wasn't just bad luck that the ice core sample was drilled at that particular spot on that day. Russ was able to have the labs in Alaska do some quick tests, under tightly controlled conditions, and sure enough, they were able to confirm that there are virus particles present in samples taken from all over the Laptev Bay area, although the viruses are far less concentrated than they were in the permafrost ice core sample that was taken on that fateful day." Everyone was silent while Drew paused and shuffled through his papers. Angela's face was grave but otherwise unreadable.

"Since there were virus particles in the other samples, we wondered why more groups working in the Arctic have not become ill. The short answer seems to be what Tally suggested last week: normally when an ice core sample is removed, it is much more solidly frozen, and it is immediately wrapped in strong plastic and insulation to reduce its contact with the air. This is so that there is no contamination of the inside with our outside atmosphere. Upon reaching the lab at the barracks, the ice core samples are kept in protective cases, and are never exposed to the open atmosphere of the barracks, even when they are analyzed. These precautions, which were created for an entirely different reason, must have also served to protect the workers. However, that doesn't entirely answer the question of why no one ever fell sick before."

Angela removed a pair of glasses from a red leather case in her purse, as well as a small notebook, and began taking notes.

"Now, before we continue, let's back up and talk about something else. We sent some e-mails to Dr. Haldor Aamodt, a Norwegian scientist whose team of researchers are the world's leading experts on Megaviridae. They were obliging and informed us that after a virus has been dormant for a long time, thousands of years in this case, lying buried under a lot of weight, its capsid can become hardened and thickened with layers of hydrocarbons. If this happens, then it is not likely that it will suddenly become virulent the moment it's removed from its icy tomb."

Sarah felt a spark of pride flicker in her chest. It was a small thing, really, but it made her feel good. When Drew had asked her that question almost two weeks ago, about whether the capsid might have undergone a biochemical change, she had suggested that he not try to re-invent the wheel by doing a lot of experiments, especially since time was such a limited commodity, but rather that he should reach out to other scientists who might have some answers. He had obviously taken her advice. She had not known about Dr. Aamodt, but she was glad that this kind stranger had responded to Drew's questions.

"Dr. Aamodt explained that in the other parts of the world where Megaviridae and Giant viruses have been discovered, it had taken some time to 'bait' the virus to draw it out. All of the virus particles found had massive capsids, so it made sense to assume that our Laptev virus may have also had a thicker coat at one time. Russ Morrison, the geologist, put us in contact with the labs at Riesigoil-Alaska that still had ice core samples from other sites that had been maintained at -70°C, and they were able to ship us a few samples in which they had detected viral particles.

"When we received the ice core samples we were able to confirm that the number of viruses per sample was much lower than the number of viruses found in the ice core sample which infected everyone. But most importantly, the virus particles found in the other ice core samples do have a thicker capsid with multiple overlapping layers of hydrocarbons over them. This means that unless there is something else present which would eat away at those hydrocarbons, thinning the layer that was formed around the capsid, these frozen viruses were not going to be imminent threats to anyone."

Angela pushed her glasses farther up her nose and scribbled another note.

"So we began doing tests on the new virus particles," said Tally. "One advantage of Laptev virus and other Megaviridae is that they are so large that it doesn't take an electron microscope to see them, as it would your average garden-variety viruses which are hundreds or thousands of times smaller."

"Yes, we've actually even gotten a visual of a few of them on a light microscope. It was so cool, though you can't make out any details at that magnification. They basically just look like a tiny bacillus shapes," added Drew.

"I still don't get it. If the viruses are surfacing all around," said Emile, "how come other groups of workers in the area haven't gotten sick? Even with thicker capsids, I mean, eventually some of them would have thinned naturally, it seems, and then caused an infection."

"Well, we wondered that too," said Drew, obviously proud to be sharing how much they had advanced in such a short time period. "We know that the Siberian permafrost has a neutral pH, which is why it's such a great medium in which DNA viruses can survive for millennia. So that gave us an idea. One of the effects of overloading our atmosphere with carbon dioxide has been the gradual acidification of the ocean. The pH hasn't changed all that much, since the ocean's saline content makes it react like a giant buffer."

"Sorry, can you remind me what a buffer is?" asked Angela, with the confidence of one whose ignorance is not linked to her pride. After all, Angela's company was paying big money for this research, and she had every right to interrupt the flow of conversation to be sure that she understood what was going on.

"A buffer is a solution that doesn't change pH when you add a bit of an acid or a bit of a base to it," said

Tally. Sarah remembered how much she loved to explain things. Perhaps she would become a professor some day. "If you have an unbuffered solution and you add some acid, the pH will drop. Buffers are especially important for living cells because a change in pH can kill them. So we work with buffers in the lab quite extensively."

"So you're saying the ocean is a buffer?" asked Angela.

"Sure. It's because of its high salt content. I can explain the intricacies of the chemistry if you want, but suffice it to say that if the ocean wasn't a buffer, life would not have begun on this planet. Another common buffer is blood."

"Okay, I'll take your word for it. Please carry on," said Angela, turning back to Drew. "You were saying something about the ocean being a buffer."

"Yes," said Drew. "So after absorbing literally tons and tons of carbon dioxide which we humans have pumped into the air for the last one hundred and fifty years, and which turns into carbonic acid when it mixes with the water, the ocean's pH has been lowered by about a tenth of a pH unit. However, if you understand the way the pH scale works, it is logarithmic, so that tiny change really means that the ocean's acidity has increased by 25%, which, not surprisingly, has been enough to wipe out entire coral reefs and kill millions of sea creatures."

"And alter the capsid of one Laptev virus strain?" asked Rhonda.

Drew and Tally nodded in unison.

"Yes ma'am," said Tally. "It turns out that one Laptev virus strain is quite sensitive to the slightly lowered pH of sea water. As modern people drill down through the melting permafrost and into the ocean for oil wells, the sea water has more of an opportunity to interact with the thawing soil."

Sarah remembered watching a documentary, just a few weeks ago, about the Arctic and how quickly everything was melting. She and John had commented on the irony of the beauty of the ice even as the glaciers diminished. Whole chunks, some the size of Manhattan, were breaking off in Greenland. All of this was before she had ever heard of Laptev and she had had no idea at the time how relevant that information would soon be.

"So we took a closer look at the situation," continued Tally, "and we decided to focus on elucidating how the ocean water was interacting with the capsid to change it." Tally nodded to Drew and he projected a large electron microscope photograph of the Laptev virus. "As you can see, it has an elongated shape with what looks like some sort of an opening at one end," she said, pointing with her pen.

"Kind of reminds me of an ancient vessel, you know, one of those you see at the museums," said Miquela.

"Actually, the technical name is amphora shaped, and you're right, Miquela, the name of the shape comes from a Greek or Roman jar," said Tally, smiling at her. Definitely a professor, thought Sarah.

"Well, I don't know about that. More than a Roman water jug, to me it kind of looks more like a corndog that someone yanked the stick out of," said Shane, irreverently.

Emile quickly shushed him, but Shane continued, unabated. "It does! I mean, take a look at those little hair thingies on the end there," he said, pointing to the top right hand corner where one part of the viral capsid did not meet the other end. "That little fringe action there. That's where the stick was before someone pulled it out.

Except it looks all empty, like they must've taken the hot dog too."

Sarah gave him a withering look and he shrugged his shoulders as if he had no idea why she could possibly be upset with him.

Drew stood up, possibly hoping to distract attention from Shane by drawing everyone's eyes to his tall, lean stature. "As it turns out," he said, his voice strong and confident, "the increased acidity of the ocean is not only changing the morphology of the capsid, removing that layer of hydrocarbons, but it's also seeping in through the lipid bilayer that lines the capsid, and reaching the viral DNA, which it primes to get it ready to infect host cells."

"Whoa, I'm sorry to interrupt again here," said Angela, making a 'time out' sign with her hands, "but you just lost me. Would you mind backtracking and saying some of that in English, please."

Tally smiled and took over the explanation. "Viruses, you see, aren't active aggressors like many pathogenic bacteria—the ones that make you sick, 'cause you know that all bacteria don't make you sick, right? People think that all bacteria are bad, and the truth is that the vast majority of them are not at all interested in eating us."

Angela smiled.

"Okay, cool, so bacteria, the pathogenic ones, they attack their way into cells, kind of like biting or tearing their way in, except, of course, they don't have mouths. But viruses, they aren't alive or anything so they can't fight their way into the cell they want to infect. Instead they mimic a chemical compound that the cell would normally take in through its membrane."

"Like a wolf in sheep's clothing," said Shane, and then changing his voice to a higher pitch he said, "Let me in, let me in, little pig, I've brought you something nice to eat."

Sarah was about to ask Shane to leave the room, but Angela chuckled and placed her hand lightly on Sarah's forearm. Sarah immediately understood that Angela was reassuring her that Shane's behavior was not bothering her. Sarah glanced at Rhonda who also gave her a small nod. They were all enjoying the conversation.

"I think I get it," said Angela, still smiling. "So you're saying that the Laptev virus, if it had never came in contact with ocean water, it might not have made anyone sick?"

Tally nodded. "Well, that's a bit of an oversimplification, but yes, that's the general drift."

"And that means," said Rhonda, "that any other drilling sites in the Arctic could still be in danger as the ocean's water could wear away at the capsids."

"Right."

"But what I don't get," said Angela, "is that the ice core sample they took wasn't from under the ocean. It was from the permafrost which was under several feet of ice. So how did salt water get in there?"

"If the ice core sample had been taken far from the coastline, perhaps there would not have been an opportunity for it to mix with ocean water, you are right. But if you look at the geology of the area," said Drew, pulling up a map of the area on his laptop screen, "the permafrost, which has been frozen for thousands of years, sits right up against the edge of the ocean. And we know the sample was thawing, which is why it broke so easily. If you look here, you can see that there's ice on the top of the ocean, but underneath, it is all melting. Russ confirmed all of this when we spoke."

Angela returned to her seat and began writing furiously in her notebook again.

"Exactly," said Tally. "As best we can tell, the crews who worked there in the previous seasons were fortunate, but their luck may not hold out. Anyway, to confirm our hypothesis that the increasingly acidic ocean water could be affecting the virus, we decided to run another experiment."

Sarah noticed Angela nod to Oscar in approval and felt a surge of gratefulness toward her investigators who were really shining in their presentations. For a completely impromptu meeting with these important people, things were going remarkably well.

"Working in a laminar flow hood in the BSL-4 lab, we isolated some virus particles and suspended them in ice, then ran a stream of ocean water over the ice. Then we exposed some HeLa cells to the viruses and measured the degree of virulence," said Tally.

"It sounds…dangerous," said Angela.

"Well, not that much, actually. The laminar flow at the entrance of the hood keeps all the microorganisms inside. And we were wearing full protective suits as well. So it was okay. But anyway, at first it didn't work. We checked all of the cells and none got infected. So the next day we repeated the experiment except we added some water vapor to the mix, and bingo! The viral particles became virulent and infected the cells. So, the fact that there's ice melting, and some of it must also sublime, you know, go straight from ice to vapor, is also important in increasing the pathogenicity of the virus."

"What was your control?" asked Rhonda. Sarah had been about to ask the same question, and as she listened, time seemed to stand still for her. She was concentrating on what was being said. Many people thought that being an investigator involved many exciting moments such as these, with stimulating and intriguing information showing up, almost unbidden, and researchers leaping to great conclusions with little or no effort.

However, the truth was much more mundane. The vast majority of the time it took long, hard hours, days, weeks, months and years, and even then, more often than not, little progress was made. Experiments which seemed like they would shed a great deal of light on the situation often gave results which instead, opened up several more paths of questioning. And that's when these experiments actually worked. All too often experiments failed when something went wrong with one of the apparatuses, or one of the ingredients in the cultivars, or, frustratingly, when the microorganisms just didn't grow and behave as expected. Then the scientist had to go back to the beginning, painstakingly checking each and every step, and repeating perhaps months of experimental work. It was arduous and wearisome and every small step forward was questioned and examined lest there were problems with the controls or interpretation of the data. Thus conversations such as these were a rare treat indeed.

"We used two different controls, just in case: ocean water at the pH it was a hundred years ago and plain water. Both do a worse job of priming the virus capsid, and afterwards, when it actually makes contact with the cells, the virus takes a lot longer to infect them or does not infect them at all. So our conclusion is that the ocean water at today's pH is doing something to the viral capsid to make it both more likely to become airborne as well as more permeable so it will be taken up more easily by the host cell," said Drew, his long fingers fiddling with one of the buttons on his lab coat.

"The next thing we did," said Tally, "was to test if perhaps part of the reason that the virus was becoming more active was due to the change in pH. So we exposed the virus to different weak acids to see if they acted on the capsid."

She tapped some keys on her laptop and pulled up another Excel worksheet filled with data. Then she scrolled down until she had several graphs on the screen. "Here, can everyone see this?" she asked, hovering the mouse's arrow over the graph that she was indicating.

Angela and Rhonda leaned in.

"We exposed the virus to different concentrations of Formic acid, Acetic acid, and Trichloroacetic acid. They did make the capsid more permeable, but not to a significant degree. So our conclusion for now is that it's not just the acidity that's having an effect on the virus, but also other components in the sea water," said Tally, using the arrow to trace the various curves outlined in the graph. The curves were in different colors, each representing one of the different acids and the buffer that they had used as the control.

Rhonda and Angela nodded as they inspected the different concentrations of acid that Tally and Drew had used. Sarah realized her team must have surrendered their weekends to be able to have so many results to discuss. She felt proud of them for their perseverance, though she would definitely have to keep her promise about insisting that everyone take some time off after they finished the work on the Laptev virus.

"Just out of curiosity, anything on the radioactive waste that Shane mentioned?" asked Sarah, turning to look at Shane.

Emile scratched his head and spoke first. "Well, we can't really say. There's certainly a huge amount of it up in the Arctic Ocean. Shane did some research…"

"Yes," said Shane who had started to raise his hand again, then caught himself and quickly lowered it. Sarah could tell he was excited to have something to contribute, and for her part, she just hoped he would keep it appropriate. "There are lots of submarines with uranium still sealed in their reactors—at least we hope they are still sealed. There are also quite a few nuclear dumps in the Kara Sea, which is right next to the Laptev Sea, just east of it. It's crazy how much sh…I mean," Shane said, blushing, "there's tons of radioactive material there. I had no idea it was so much."

"And Russ said that there are several oil companies planning to drill there, in the Kara Sea, I mean, in the near future. It's quite a remote region, but you never know. It would be just their luck to go to drill and end up disturbing one of those toxic reservoirs," said Drew.

Sarah saw Angela's face darken at the mention of other oil companies. Obviously Drew's comment had hit a sore spot. Then Oscar leaned over and whispered something to Angela. She shook her head and said in a soft voice, "No, we're not going into the Kara Sea."

"That's smart," said Shane, shamelessly addressing Oscar. "I'd stay the…I mean, well, I wouldn't recommend going anywhere near there. I also discovered that there were a ton of 'secret dumps.' Reports that I read said there were 17,000 containers and more than a dozen ships with radioactive waste, and something like 14 nuclear reactors. The Russians have been dumping stuff up there for decades, pretty much unchecked."

"Damn!" said Oscar, his brow surging skyward in surprise.

"Yeah," said Shane, obviously enjoying himself once again. "It's a ticking time bomb up there. I think they began dumping in the 1950s. And after all that time you know there's gonna be stuff leaking, if there hasn't already been stuff released. Things don't stay put, you know. Not under those conditions, with the salt and the pressure of the weight of all that water. The ocean erodes things and all metal eventually succumbs."

"I guess we're lucky that Laptev didn't make its debut earlier, given the conditions in that part of the world," said Miquela.

Everyone in the group nodded grimly.

"The thing is," said Drew, "the fact that this Laptev virus was there in the first place, and that it was able to make humans sick, is significant. It may be that the acidic ocean permeated the capsid and activated the virus, but if you gave ocean water to a virus that doesn't generally affect humans, it's not going to suddenly make someone sick. So, this Laptev virus most likely did see humans in the past."

"And that's what Tally was saying earlier, with the ancient humans chasing the mammoths around, right?" said Rhonda.

"Hold on," said Angela. "Sorry, guys, I meant to ask earlier, but I just want to clarify. So if a virus has never made humans sick before, then it's not a danger to us now?"

"Generally speaking, yes, that's right," said Sarah.

"But, I don't get it," said Angela. "It had to have started with one human in the first place, right? I mean, it's the old chicken and the egg problem. So why are you all so sure that Laptev *had* to have infected people in the past?"

"You can think of it as a numbers game," said Rhonda, her deep voice commanding the attention of everyone in the room. "With the way the workers got sick, you know, so many within a few hours of touching the ice, it makes it extremely unlikely that the virus had *not* seen a human host before. As we were saying earlier, viruses aren't active aggressors. They need the 'key' to get inside the locked door of the cell membrane in the first place. If Laptev had never seen humans, then it would not have been able to 'unlock' human cells so quickly and make so many people sick. The fact that Laptev was so virulent so quickly is *proof* that it must have already known how to infect humans."

Angela looked doubtful.

"You know how once you've solved a tricky puzzle you're more likely to get it right faster the next time you see it?" asked Miquela, blushing slightly.

"Sure, the whole 'key' thing," said Angela. "But I still don't think it makes sense."

"Okay, so then let's take it to a higher level," she said, turning redder with each word. "If you have a team trying to go through an obstacle course, and they get to a series of puzzles that only one person knows how to solve, it's going to take a while for that person to work with all the members of the team to show them how to solve it. But if the team has a bunch of people who have all seen that type of puzzle before, they're going to resolve it quicker."

"Got it," said Angela, smiling.

Tally picked up the thread of the conversation again. "So, that raised another question which was: where did the virus come from in the first place, meaning, how did it get in the ice? It's a pretty aggressive pathogen, so it probably did not exist in all human populations. Otherwise they would have all been decimated or perhaps we would have evolved with the virus and over the years, built up more immunity. So it makes sense that the Laptev was probably somehow more localized to that area. It's a bit of long shot, but here's what we came up with. We can assume that the early people who were in the area were probably taken ill with the virus. That pretty much has to be a given or otherwise there's no explanation for how the virus would suddenly become so toxic to humans. But, where did these early people get it from?"

"That's my question exactly," said Angela, pointing a finger at Tally.

"When we explained about the mammoths migrating through the Laptev Bay area last week, we guessed that this theory was probably right and these early people were likely following them, hunting for food. Many tribes of nomads did that, so it makes a lot of sense. So it occurred to us that maybe the mammoths were carrying the virus, and perhaps when the prehistoric people killed the giant animals to eat them, they became infected in turn. And that's when Drew had a brilliant idea."

"I don't know about brilliant," said Drew, blushing slightly. "I just wondered if modern Asian elephants might also be carriers of the virus, you know, since they are the living species that is most closely related to the mammoth. I wasn't sure if anyone had ever looked at those elephants that way. I mean, especially if the virus was silent, then perhaps it could have been present in the elephant's tissues and no one would have noticed it."

"Perhaps," said Rhonda, placing the tips of her fingers on her chin pensively. "It does seem like a reasonable thing to take a look at."

"So we contacted an elephant reserve in northern Asia," said Tally.

"I have a friend who speaks Cantonese and she translated for us," said Drew.

"And they sent us some tissue samples from several different animals, old and young," concluded Tally.

Sarah was glad that these two were sitting next to one another or it would have been like watching a tennis match, having to keep swiveling her head between the speakers. As it was, she only had to flick her eyes back and forth.

"Well?" said Rhonda, obviously barely able to contain herself. "What did you find? Are they carriers?"

Sarah realized that if the elephants were found to carry the virus, this would be a tremendously important breakthrough. Prior to the recent macabre discovery that the Laptev virus had the ability to infect humans, there were no documented cases of Megaviridae affecting anything larger than an amoeba. Indeed, it was only in the last ten years that giant viruses had been discovered, all in remote locations of the planet, and she did not know if anyone had ever searched for them inside animal cells.

Sarah thought about Asian elephants for a moment. What did she know about them? Human efforts were largely centered on trying to protect them from poachers who supplied profligate wealthy avarices who had an insatiable appetite for ivory. Thus these large mammals were on the verge of extinction. But how much was known about their physiology? Could it be that these pachyderms carried a hidden stowaway? Might they harbor a large, hitherto obscure virus, a vestige from their furrier ancestors? It would certainly be an interesting twist.

Tally grimaced and said, "No, unfortunately the Asian elephants do not appear to be carrying the virus."

Sarah let out a breath that she didn't realize she had been holding, and closed her eyes. Another dead end.

"Furthermore, when we cultured the Asian elephant cells and introduced the virus, it did not seem to parasitize the cells the way we would have expected," Drew said. "The tests aren't conclusive yet, of course, but our initial trials seem to indicate that the virus enters the cells and integrates into the chromosomal DNA, but does not produce an outright infection. Instead it just kind of rides along, not growing, and not bothering the cells."

"A latent virus," said Emile.

"Maybe that's how it infected the humans," added Miquela, who was also being carried away with the excitement of the conversation. "Maybe the virus was just hanging out in the woolly mammoths and then when the humans killed it, they became contaminated."

"Well, I hesitate to agree," said Drew, running his long fingers through his hair. "My understanding is that even latent viruses *do*, at some point, become active and virulent. And maybe Laptev viruses in the elephant cells will eventually become virulent as well, under conditions we have yet to assess, but for now, the virus just behaves itself, staying put and not giving the elephant cells any reason to fear it."

"Maybe it would have infected woolly mammoths, but these Asian elephants are different enough genetically that the virus doesn't really do anything to them," suggested Emile.

Tally raised an eyebrow and nodded. Drew seemed preoccupied with another screen and was tapping away at the laptop.

Sarah nodded slowly as she thought about the idea. She had to admit that she was intrigued. "So, let me see, if I understand correctly then, based on the excellent work you two have done in the last three weeks, and the information Emile, Shane and Miquela have also gathered, our working theory is that in this particular basin, the Laptev virus was present in unusually large concentrations in the ice cores, possibly because it was carried in human cells and perhaps, but not necessarily, mammoth cells as well at some point in the ancient past. Then something happened: perhaps there was a mass extermination event or something."

"Polar bears attacked! And they slaughtered everyone in a ten mile radius. The blood soaked into the icy ground and the virus became frozen in time," said Shane, who was so excited that a small drop of saliva flew from his mouth as he spoke.

Sarah didn't know whether to smack him for interrupting or laugh it off. In the end she chose to just carry on talking as if he had not said anything. "Whatever the reason, the virus froze in the layers of snow and ice and then went into hibernation, so to speak, and over the years its capsid was covered with thick layers of hydrocarbons. When the drilling began, the virus was exposed to the more acidic sea water, which made changes to the capsid. Between that and the ice sheet melting, there were a series of bad coincidences, including the bear attack, which then led to the virus becoming more volatile and being released easily from the crushed ice sample. It then immediately contaminated the crew who was working there.

When they got back to the lab, the unsuspecting lab personnel, knowing that the ice core sample had been basically ruined for the delicate studies to which it would normally have been subjected, worked on the ice without due protection, and consequently they too became infected. Then Laptev spread through the air every time someone coughed or sneezed, like the flu virus does, and because of the icy gale, no one could radio for help or leave the compound. Basically, the conditions were ripe for the perfect storm."

"Okay, this is good. You all have done wonderful work," Rhonda said, and clapped a bit. She was joined by Oscar and Angela who each applauded a few times. Sarah also raised her hands, clapping for her team.

"Okay, how about the mice?" Sarah asked. "Any news on experiments with them?"

"We've infected several groups and we are running different tests. I'm afraid it will be a few more days before we have some answers," said Emile. "We'd like to report on them in next week's meeting."

"Great," said Sarah, ready to be done with the meeting. "We'll adjourn then for the week. Please keep me abreast of any new developments, and meanwhile, let's all carry on and see what else we can learn."

CHAPTER 10

"We'll keep this one succinct," Rhonda assured Sarah as they headed down the hallway. "I know you've got work to do."

Sarah had walked out of the lab to say goodbye to Rhonda, Oscar and Angela who had crashed her meeting with her researchers. The meeting had gone tremendously well, and she was eager to get back to her work, but now suddenly she was being drawn into another meeting, this time up in Rhonda's office. Sarah's earlier apprehension returned. She wondered about the purpose of the meeting—was Rhonda going to change her mind and insist that she and her team continue studying the Laptev virus for a longer period than the initial six weeks she had promised? Perhaps that is why Angela and Oscar had joined the meeting, to put their weight behind the new proposal?

She thought about it as she walked slowly to the elevator. Oscar, Angela and Rhonda were a few paces ahead, engrossed in conversation which she didn't really mind missing. Well, the truth was that it might not be such an imposition on her lab after all if that is what they wanted to do. Her team was making terrific progress and clearly there were many more questions that could be answered by extending the project for several more months. With the rapid pace of their investigations thus far, they just might be able to discover some truly remarkable things about Laptev if they had more time.

When Sarah reached Rhonda's office, the others were seated in chairs that were much more comfortable than the lab stools had been.

"Thanks, everyone," said Angela. "Sarah, I'm astounded with the research you all have done so far. You have a remarkable team. They are witty, dynamic and definitely engaging. I'll admit that I didn't understand every single thing that they said, but I got the gist of it and I'll be happy to report back to my CEO, Stan Sundback, that Riesigoil's money is being well spent."

Sarah accepted the compliment and the warm smiles that Rhonda and Oscar directed at her. She was more certain now that Angela would be saying something about extending the project. It was the only thing that made sense given the circumstances.

"Now, what I've got to say isn't easy," continued Angela. "I'm going to be frank with you all because what I'm about to say will also impact you, although to a lesser extent. You won't be surprised to hear that as HSE VP, I cannot, in good conscience, authorize continued drilling in that part of the Arctic, even on a temporary basis."

Sarah nodded. It was clear that the virus was still out there, and it was in more parts of the ice than they had originally known about. Authorizing a return to that part of the Arctic would be madness.

"However, if we cannot continue with our Arctic exploration, that leaves us, my company, in a quandary. We've spent a lot of money to set up machinery for drilling, and the shareholders are getting anxious about profits that will be lost if another company gets their wells in that area into production before we do."

Angela paused and everyone remained silent, waiting for her to continue.

"And if the shareholders pull out, Riesigoil will fail."

Oscar looked down at the floor and Rhonda fidgeted in her chair.

"So you're saying that if Riesigoil fails, there won't be any more grant money either," said Rhonda.

Angela nodded.

"It's a lose-lose situation," said Sarah in a soft voice. All of the joy she had derived from the advances that her team was making was now seeping out of her, as if someone had poked her balloon with a dull needle.

"Yes, unfortunately," said Angela, smiling wryly and tracing the border of Rhonda's desk with her finger, slowly dragging it back and forth. Then she looked at Sarah and said, "I wasn't exaggerating when I said that I was impressed by the work your lab is doing, but what I need to know is: do you have any idea how long it will take you all to come up with some answers that will allow for drilling to begin again?"

All eyes were focused on Sarah who shifted, trying to find a more comfortable position for her leg which had begun throbbing right after she left the lab. She took a deep breath to stall for another moment and gather her thoughts. She had not expected to be confronted so directly, and in front of Rhonda and Oscar, no less.

"Well," she said, "we are definitely making progress at a far faster rate than I had dared to hope, but, I'm sorry. We still don't have any way of dealing with the virus once it has been contracted, and I think that's the biggest stumbling block now. As you heard, we know for sure that it's transmitted through the air, which makes it the most difficult type of virus to protect yourself from.

"Theoretically if the crews always wore Military Issue gas masks with filters for airborne virus protection, which also cover the eyes because they could also be a portal of entry, that would protect the workers, but we don't know if, since it's such a large virus, it could settle on dust particles and thus be carried on outside gear and become airborne when that gear was removed. If the virus is as persistent as the measles virus, which lingers in the air for quite a while, it would mean that enhanced protective devices would have to be worn for much longer and by more of the personnel. I really can't say for sure until we complete more studies. It's a tricky situation."

Angela frowned. "I was afraid you might say something like that."

Sarah met her eyes and saw the anxiety in them. She hated to give bad news, but she felt that she needed to be as honest as she could in her assessment. "Also, as you just heard in the meeting, we've found out that the ocean's increased acidity plays a role in activating the virus. The pH of the ocean is not something we can easily change. And with the Arctic ice melting so quickly now, it would be nearly impossible to ensure that no ocean water came into contact with the virus."

Angela nodded, obviously not thrilled with what she was hearing, but she seemed to understand. She pursed her lips and several sets of concentric wrinkles formed on each side of them, as if her dissatisfaction was rippling away from her frown across the previously pristine surface of her cheeks.

"How soon do you think your team could have this information? Or at least a few more of these answers," Angela asked.

Sarah looked at Rhonda who met her eyes briefly, then looked away. She realized with a little surprise that Rhonda did not want to confront Oscar or Angela. With her years of experience at the CDC she was in a much more credible position than Sarah to explain why there were no more answers yet and that research was a wild, unpredictable venture which often left investigators with little progress for years. Why was she leaving Sarah to do the dirty work?

Then, with sudden clarity, Sarah understood. Rhonda was afraid to lose her job. She studied her face again and saw the lines, well hidden by her carefully coiffed hair which was dyed to a perfect chestnut brown color. Her dark complexion also helped to hide her age. Thinking back to when she had read Rhonda's extensive résumé, Sarah realized that her boss was probably in her late 50s or early 60s, though she looked younger. If she lost this job, she might not easily get another.

So it was up to her to be the bad guy. Her leg suddenly throbbed again, but she swallowed and faced Angela.

"I'm really sorry, Angela, but for now, I don't know what else I can tell you. I don't have any way of predicting when we will know enough to be able to ensure that the conditions for drilling and exploration are safe. My strong recommendation would be not to allow anyone to return to that site until we know more."

Oscar raised his impressive eyebrows and brought his hands together. The meeting was over. "Well, I'm sure

Sarah will let us all know as soon as her lab gets some more answers. And given the outstanding progress they've already made, I'm sure that won't take too long," he said, his voice suddenly brisk. He stood and, after thanking Sarah and Rhonda, he escorted Angela out of the office.

Sarah looked at Rhonda, who shrugged her shoulders. "I don't know either," she said in a soft voice, not meeting Sarah's eye.

"Well, I guess I'd better get back to the lab," said Sarah, half hoping Rhonda would ask her to stay for a few more minutes. Instead, the phone rang and Sarah heard Rhonda's voice regain its former strength as she answered it and nodded a quick goodbye to Sarah. The busy and confident boss had returned, leaving no trace of the frightened older woman she had briefly glimpsed.

CHAPTER 11

Sarah looked up from her laptop and watched her husband across the table as he focused on his work. They were sitting in the kitchen, eating slices of Papa John's pizza from the box. On these nights they didn't even use paper plates to eat, they just grabbed the slices and tore off paper towels from a roll they kept in the center of the table. John absently reached for the packet of spicy pepper seeds and sprinkled it over his slice. Then in a practiced maneuver, he rolled up the slice so it looked more like a rotund croissant, turned it on its end and took a bite of the end. As he did so he looked up and caught her eye.

"What?" he said, a smile playing on his lips.

"I don't get how you can eat it that way, Dr. Chadwick," she said, also smiling. They often teased one another this way, calling each other by their honorific titles and separate last names. It was an endearing game which had begun when people—her mother in particular—had been horrified to learn that she was not willing to give up her last name when she got married. "But 'Chadwick' is a much nicer last name than 'Spallanzani,' dear," her mother had insisted.

She had harped on and on about how nice John's last name sounded until Sarah had finally tired of it. "Are you saying that if your maiden name had been 'Chadwick' you would not have taken Dad's name?" Sarah had asked. It was a low blow, but it had worked and the discussion had been dropped.

John chuckled at her teasing about the way he ate his pizza and then looked down at his screen and frowned at it.

"Something wrong?" asked Sarah, taking a bite of her own slice which she held with two hands, keeping it parallel to the table. The slice was hot enough that it burned the tips of her fingers, but she loved to eat her food scaldingly hot. She took a bite and relished pulling the long strands of gooey cheese away.

"I've got a series of results from the last two weeks of testing with these mice, and they just don't make any sense."

Sarah picked at some more strands of cheese and wrapped them around the tip of her slice, then dipped the slice in the warm garlic butter. "Why, what's up?" she asked.

She and John regularly discussed their research problems even though they were in different lines of study. It was one of the many things she loved about being married to him—that they had regular opportunities to share in each other's research details. Many of her colleagues had married people who were in disparate lines of work—they were engineers or musicians or architects, and so they did not have the luxury of discussing the intricacies of their investigations with their partners. Not that any of them seemed to mind. But Sarah relished both hearing about John's work, so foreign and different from her own, as well as sharing hers.

John shook his head. "It's really strange. The data is not what it ought to be. I mean, these mice are just not behaving the way they should."

Sarah watched as he opened his mouth wide to take another bite of the pizza roll, holding it gingerly so that the sauce wouldn't all squeeze out of the other end.

"Remember how…" he said with his mouth still full. Then he reached for a paper towel and held it over his mouth with his left hand, while he held up his right hand, palm outward like a traffic cop stopping a kid at an intersection. He quickly chewed and swallowed.

"Sorry," he said sheepishly. "Remember how I told you we were doing these anger- and fear-analysis studies for this new project with Stanford? Well, these initial tests are not really that new and we pretty much know, or can guess, how the mice will react when they are presented with a new, potentially frightening stimulus. We were just running some routine tests to establish a baseline, and then we were going to begin the actual research experiments. But first we always have to make sure that all of the different groups are reacting similarly, you know."

It was common practice to set up baselines and standards. All scientists needed to do this to be sure that the results were valid.

"Well for some strange reason, the mice in our studies are not acting afraid of the stimulus. It's quite puzzling," he said.

"Yeah?" she said, reaching for her husband's bottle of Shiner Bock beer and taking a small sip. "Maybe they've met the stimulus earlier?"

John scratched his chin thoughtfully. "I thought about that, and I checked their charts. They haven't been used for any other behavioral studies."

Sarah furrowed her eyebrows and reached for the carton of salad. "What about the handler? Could he or she have perhaps done something differently to them?"

"Actually, now that you mention it, we *do* have a different handler. A young woman, Molly, I think, is her name. I haven't actually met her yet, but she's been filling in occasionally for the last couple of months."

"Molly Greenburg?" asked Sarah, wiping her hands on a paper towel. "Oh, I really like her. She's great with the little ones. She's a regular for us. Kevin swears that the mice behave better when she tends to them. I wonder what she's doing in your section of the vivarium?"

"It would seem that Trevor, our usual handler, has a huge project for his grad classes. I guess she must need the extra hours. So she's been covering for him."

"You know, I've heard that mice behave differently depending on whether it's a male or a female who's handling them," she said, pointing at him with her crust.

John had finished his slice and reached for another, sprinkling on the hot seeds as he spoke. "Oh, I don't know about that. Do you think they can tell whether it's a male or a female who's feeding them? And why would they even care?"

"No, it's true. I read a report saying that male handlers made the mice more nervous, and could even lead to results that were quite different from those expected if the mice weren't feeling anxiety. So maybe since the handler has changed, they feel so relaxed that they aren't reacting to things that would normally make them afraid."

John scowled. "Well, maybe in some situations, but Trevor is gentle. I've seen him with them. And he has a lot of experience since he's been doing this since he was an undergrad. Plus, I still don't think it could possibly make a difference. But in any case, something is definitely wrong. I've got this one group that's acting differently from the rest. All of the mice in that group seem to be drawn to the corner of the cage where we sprinkled some drops of cat urine. It's really odd because they should be shrinking away from that corner."

"Maybe they just like the smell of urine?"

"No, I mean, maybe they do, who knows, but it doesn't make any sense. We put other types of urine in the cage too. We have one corner with cow urine, one with dog, and one with bear urine. All the groups stay far away from the corner with the cat's urine, but not this group. Every mouse in that group goes and hangs out in the corner with the cat's pee. They don't like any of the other urine smells, just the cat's. I don't get it!"

Sarah closed the pizza box, which was now empty, and walked it over to the plastic Fiesta grocery store bag that they kept for their trash. It was hanging on the inside of the cupboard door, just under the sink. She dropped the box to the floor and stepped on it carefully with her good foot to squash it, while holding onto the cabinet to keep her balance. It would not do to hurt her ankle again. Then she retrieved it and folded it a couple of times so that it would fit in the small brown plastic bag. She stuffed it in and then closed the door and returned to the table.

"I don't know. Are the mice younger or older than the others? Is there a chance that they've all lost their sense of smell for some reason? Or could the researcher have mixed up the urine samples for that group?"

"All good questions, my dear Dr. S.," said John, now getting up and walking to the freezer. He stood there another minute, then pulled out a pint of Graeter's coconut chocolate almond ice cream, which he held up for Sarah to see. She grinned and he walked to the pantry for cones. It was their Friday night tradition. "Well, we'll look into it some more on Monday."

CHAPTER 12

"Have a seat, thanks for coming up here. How's your leg?" asked Rhonda. Then, without giving Sarah a chance to answer, she dove into the rest of her thought. "Listen, I know I just asked a few days ago, but, how is that research coming along?"

Sarah could hear the strain in Rhonda's voice. Apparently the weekend had been too short for her.

"We're still making pretty good progress, but nothing really new to report since last Thursday," said Sarah. After Rhonda had dropped in on her meeting unannounced last week, Sarah had promised to continue to update her in a timely manner. But it was only Monday, so not much had happened in the lab. If Rhonda continued asking for updates every two days, Sarah thought, it would quickly become annoying.

Rhonda sighed. "I just spoke with Angela at Riesigoil. Apparently the shareholders are putting some heavy pressure on her to open the area back up for drilling."

Sarah crossed her arms. She remembered how Angela had seemed pretty desperate. Apparently the CEO was waiting for Angela to give the thumbs up in order for drilling operations to go forward. Was Angela afraid that the CEO would become impatient with her? Surely she would have told him about her meeting at the university and the progress that Sarah and her team were making?

"She said that it was her decision, as the VP of Health and Safety, right?" asked Sarah. "She won't agree to allow the company to go back there yet, will she? Not until we find out more about how to protect the workers from the Laptev virus."

Rhonda let out a slow breath and Sarah noticed the dark makeup around her eyes was slightly smudged, as if even those hard lines were becoming tired.

"I don't know, Sarah. I mean, I'm sure she certainly doesn't want to. She knows the threat is still out there and she doesn't want the company to lose any more people. The problem is that an inordinate amount of capital has been invested. And that much money can make people crazy." Rhonda was silent for a moment, and then she said, "Angela told us that there is another company drilling in the area, I guess not that far away, and the shareholders are worried that the other company will find the petroleum reserves first."

Sarah nodded. "But, surely Riesigoil owns the mineral rights of the land that they've staked out around Laptev Bay?"

"Like I said, there's an awful lot of money in this. People don't play fair when there's that much money involved. Never have, never will. The way she was explaining it," said Rhonda, a note of frustration seeping into her voice, "when companies drill nowadays, they rarely ever go straight down. They tunnel sideways, feeling with sensors located at the tips of the drilling instruments, and turning one way or the other depending on what they find. It's quite different from the way things used to be. So it's entirely possible that even if the main oil field is directly under the land that Riesigoil has staked out, someone from another company will reach the field before they do, and if so, they could have the well almost dry before Riesigoil gets to it. And that would mean a loss of billions, with a capital 'B', dollars."

"I see," said Sarah. She was quiet for a moment as she thought. Her team was definitely making progress, but it was nearly impossible to expect to resolve such a huge problem as the one the virus presented in just a few weeks. They had been fortunate to make so much progress thus far, but that was no guarantee that they would continue to fare so well. In research, one never knew how long it would take to discover answers.

"Now I know that this type of research normally takes much longer," said Rhonda, as if she was reading Sarah's thoughts. "I think I told you that three and a half weeks ago when the project first started. We don't need to crack the nut wide open, Sarah. We just need to get far enough along that we can recommend that the site be re-opened in a safe manner."

Sarah looked down at the moon boot on her sore ankle and gently raised it a few inches, contemplating the large black Velcro bands that held her foot captive. "Well, we're not that far along yet," she said quietly.

Rhonda pursed her lips in a resigned fashion. "I understand, believe me, and I'm pleased with the progress your group has made thus far. But let me remind you that half of the time allotted for this project has now elapsed. We are in the fourth week, and Angela is expecting further progress before long. Oscar is too. And so am I."

Sarah let out a sigh. She hated the pressure, but it was inherent in a situation like this one, where people had lost their lives. "I'll talk to the team again this afternoon," she said, "and I'll let you know as soon as something new is found. That's the best I can do, Rhonda."

Sarah ran her hand over her ponytail, smoothing it out in a distracted manner. She was glad that she did not have Angela's position at the oil company. She was sure that it paid far better than what she earned at the university, but the stress was also commensurately higher.

CHAPTER 13

When she returned to her office, Sarah opened the file of data that Emile had compiled on the most recent mice experiments and began scanning the results. The data was still crude and they would need to process it by applying several statistical tests to the numbers to be sure the results were reliable before any of them could be discussed or shared. Still, with the progress they had made so far, she was fairly certain that the results they were seeking would soon be within her grasp.

She stared at the tables and graphs for about fifteen minutes, but the data didn't seem to be pointing to any immediate conclusions. She shook her head and closed her eyes. If only there was more information about the Laptev virus in the first place. Good scientists always stood on the shoulders of other good scientists. If there was more data available, she might be able to make a link, some connection that would tip the scales in the learning process. She opened another browser and typed a few words into a search engine when suddenly there was a knock at her office door. For a second she imagined that it was Rhonda, coming to tell her some more bad news, but then Emile opened the office door and peeked around the edge of it.

"Come on in," said Sarah with more good humor than she felt, and then seeing his sagging shoulders and the look of distress on his face as he grasped his notebook tightly, she quietly asked what the matter was.

Emile cleared his throat and said, "I'm afraid we have some really bad news."

Sarah reached for the lid of her laptop and lowered it, giving Emile her full attention. "What is it?" she asked, her voice cracking slightly and her heart pounding loudly in her chest as various scenarios flashed in quick succession across her mind. Had one of the investigators become ill with the Laptev virus? That was the worst-case scenario and it had played in the back of her mind and haunted her dreams nearly every night since the investigations began. She absolutely dreaded the thought of having any of her team become ill, or worse.

In an attempt to assuage her fears she had asked that the Environmental Health and Safety Department of the university re-examine all of the protective equipment before her team began working with the virus, and she had called for regular inspections at intervals that were more frequent than those recommended by the manufacturer. She had also continued to stress the importance of safety habits at every turn. She didn't want to take any chances and she preferred to have her team angry or bored with her repetitions rather than ever feel remorse that she could have done more.

"I'm sorry but I think you'd better come have a look at the mice results. I think there's been some sort of a mistake and…" Emile didn't finish his thought.

Sarah's pulse settled a bit. At least no one was injured. But what had gone wrong with the experiments? Why was he looking so upset? She stifled the tirade of questions which began to flood her mind.

"I've got your data pulled up," said Sarah, raising the lid of her laptop.

Emile approached her desk and quickly found a graph that she had not yet inspected.

"You see, I just created another graph while I was analyzing the data," he said, pointing to some brightly colored lines with a capped pen that he removed from his lab coat. "So if you look here and here. These mice should, in theory, have the exact same reaction to the invading virus as these guys over here, but as you can see, their reactions are quite different."

Sarah inspected the data, her eyes darting back and forth across the page as comprehension dawned upon her. Yes, the disparity between the groups was tremendous. It was definitely not an expected result.

"So these mice have had different treatments? Did they get different batches of virus?"

Emile shook his head. "They had different dosages, yes, but all from the same batch."

Sarah clicked between the two graphs again, trying to see if there could be an explanation. "Maybe the quantities that they received were inaccurately recorded?"

"No, that's the thing. Even within groups that had the same quantity, the results are mixed up. They all had the same batch of virus. Their reactions should be...more predictable, and they are clearly *not*. This group here, for example, had a high dosage of virus, and that group there had a miniscule dosage. And look what's happened."

Sarah shook her head. "But, that's not possible," she said. "These over here with the high dosage have all survived and these that hardly got any virus are almost all dead. Are you sure the groups weren't mislabeled?"

Emile shook his head while he bit the inside of his cheeks. "We did the experiments in triplicate and there were two people checking. The labels are correct."

"Maybe the mice were switched somehow," she said, still refusing to believe the results in front of her eyes.

"No. At first we thought maybe the vivarium had given us the wrong mice, you know, maybe they had mixed them up and given us ones with some mutation built in or something, so we asked them to double check and eventually we asked them for all their paperwork."

"And?" said Sarah, desperately trying to come up with a rational explanation. Perhaps the mice had some sort of mutation which would make their immune system weaker, and they would not be able to defend themselves as well from an infection?

"No, they gave us only animals that they had labeled as 'Wildtype', which is what we wanted. But the results make no sense."

"When did you realize this?" asked Sarah.

Emile looked down at his immaculately kept notebook and flipped the pages. "I began suspecting that something might be going wrong a couple of days ago, but it wasn't until last night, when I got all of the data plotted, that I could really see that something was amiss."

Working late on Sunday night, thought Sarah briefly. It didn't surprise her. If it were not for her injured ankle she would probably also have been putting in some weekend appearances.

"And then, of course, when I got in this morning we found a lot of dead ones, especially from the lowest dosage group, which is what you are seeing here. I showed the information to Drew and Shane, and we began running some quick biochemical tests on the tissue samples from both sets of mice. And we've extracted some DNA."

"You were trying to see if there is a genetic difference between them that would explain their reactions," said Sarah, thinking aloud. She was annoyed that Emile had not come to her immediately, but she now saw that he and the others had taken the same steps that she would have recommended.

"Yes, but we can't find a difference. The mice are all clearly from the same gene pool."

"Call the labs that supply the mice. See if they can verify the lineage."

Emile nodded. Sarah began clicking through more screens, looking at the various graphs and comparing the results from the different groups of mice. It was obvious that Emile was right—these mice should have had predictable reactions to the viral infection, but that was clearly not the case. In some cases the high dosage of virus killed the mice, and in some it did not. In some groups the low dosage killed the mice, and in others, it did not. The results made no sense.

"And did you put some tissue samples under the microscope to see if the virus was present in the mice that are still alive?" asked Sarah.

"No," said Emile, "but I'll get right on it."

"Okay, let's see what the mouse supplier says and what the tissue samples show us. I'm going to go speak with Kevin and see if he might remember anything from when he got us the mice."

When Sarah left her office she headed down the hall to where the techs generally worked. It was a smaller room, and since many of the techs were undergraduate students, they often brought their class work and sat at tables when there was not too much going on in the main lab. She was glad that it was not a distant walk. Her leg was beginning to ache again. As she entered the room, Sarah scanned the tables and quickly found Kevin sitting close to a window, poking away at his phone.

"Kevin," she said, once she had wrested his attention from the monopolizing device. "We seem to have a problem with mice we're using for these new experiments."

Kevin looked at her blankly.

"The *mice*," she repeated. "The mice you got us for the experiments for the Laptev virus. Something is wrong with them."

Kevin raised an eyebrow as his expression changed to a slightly different kind of confused.

Sarah closed her eyes, realizing this was a task that she should have delegated. She had far too many problems to be speaking with this young man who seemed to have no life outside of his phone. She tried once more, this time conveying her ideas in staccato thoughts that he might be able to grasp before his mind wandered.

"The mice are reacting discordantly to the same stimulus. They should all have the same reaction. It doesn't make sense. I'd like you to check with the people who work in the vivarium and see if you can find anything that might give us a clue as to why the mice are acting differently. Anything at all. Do you think you could have an answer for me by tomorrow?"

Kevin nodded and Sarah decided that that was good enough.

CHAPTER 14

The next morning Sarah met with her group of researchers again. "As you all know by now," she said, "we seem to have a problem with our mice here, and it could be egregious. Emile, Drew and Shane have run several tests using the mice as hosts for the Laptev virus, and there seems to be a discrepancy in the control group. Some of them contract the viral infection and die, while others contract it and live perfectly well. And the dosage we gave them, which should affect the rate of infection and illness, seems to not have the expected result."

She paused and a furrow creased her brow. "So far we cannot find a pattern, and it certainly makes no sense that if the mice were all identical to begin with, there would be such differing reactions to the virus. I've asked several of you to follow up with some further investigations, and I'd like for all of us to pay close attention to see if between us we can crack this nut. Emile, will you please begin"

Emile nodded. "We took samples from striated muscles, as well as different organs, to see if there was a difference between the mice that lived, which we've called the ML's, and the ones that didn't make it, which we're calling the MBD's."

"MBD's, right," said Shane, chuckling under his breath as if he was just getting a joke. "I just love that name."

There were a few more giggles from Tally and Miquela and then Emile said, "It was Drew's idea."

Sarah was amused, in spite of herself. "Drew, would you like to share what that acronym means?" asked Sarah, a small smile playing on her lips.

All eyes turned to Drew and he said, "Well, okay, it was a hasty decision." When no one responded after a few more seconds he said. "All right! Don't get bent out of shape. It stands for Mice that Bit the Dust, okay?"

Everyone chuckled for a moment and then Emile continued with his account. "We preserved the dead mice as soon as we found them, to prevent tissue breakdown that might impair our ability to see what was going on. We took the samples in triplicate, fixed and stained them and examined them early this morning."

"In most tissues and organs, we saw no difference between the two groups. However, if you'll click on the picture there," said Drew, indicating a file that revealed an enlarged photograph. "We were almost through examining the tissue samples when we got to the brain tissue slide. Since we hadn't seen any differences so far on any of the other organs or the muscle tissue, we were planning to do an ELISA assay with the blood, using antibodies from human HeLa cells to detect the presence of the virus, but before we even got to that, we saw this."

Here Drew stopped and pointed to a dark circular shape with the tip of his pencil.

Sarah glanced at the slides of tissue projected on the screen. She saw that in some of the mice, the regularly shaped pink cells of the brain, long and sinuous, had large, dark purple circles inside the main body of the cell, with lots of dark little dots. She raised her eyebrows in surprise and asked "What are those? They're not supposed to be there, are they?"

Emile shook his head, no. "I'm not certain what they are, but some of the mice have them and some don't. Whatever they are, they don't seem to be having a negative health effect on the mice. They look and act perfectly normal. No changes in eating, sleeping or learning behavior."

For a moment everyone sat there looking at the translucent, pink images of brain cells on the slides on the screen. The purple dots were not in all the slides, but from what Sarah knew, they should not have been in any of them.

Sarah sat back and crossed her arms as the full impact of what she had been told began to sink in. Those little dark purple dots were definitely a problem. A humongous problem.

Or maybe she was jumping to premature conclusions. Perhaps if they had only taken samples from the dead mice, the dots could have been a product of metabolic decay. "You took these samples from living mice as well?" she asked.

"Yeah, this picture on the screen is from a biopsy of a living animal," he said.

Sarah felt her shoulders tightening. "So the results that we have gathered over the past several weeks with the mice are pretty much meaningless?" she asked, already knowing the answer.

Emile and Drew kept their eyes fixed on the image of the brain cells on the screen, but Emile's face was drained of color.

Sarah closed her eyes and shook her head. "I don't believe it! Could there be a mistake? Maybe the slides were dirty before the mounts were made..." It was a lame suggestion, she knew. The dots were clearly stained with the same dye as the cells and there was no way that they could be random dust motes.

"We've double and triple checked," said Drew, obviously as frustrated as Sarah and Emile. "There's no doubt that some of the control mice are contaminated. And whatever has contaminated those mice is definitely there in those brain cells."

Sarah felt like she would burst from frustration. She had just spoken with Rhonda the day before, assuring her of their progress and now this had happened.

Emile and Drew returned their gazes to the floor. Even Shane had the good sense to keep quiet.

"Well, some of the mice weren't contaminated," said Drew. "Some of the samples from the dead mice..."

Sarah whirled on him. "Oh, I guess that should make me feel better? How many, perchance, would you say, were clean?"

"We, eh, we don't have exact numbers," stammered Emile.

Sarah shook her head. "Four *weeks*. Four of our six weeks' worth of experiments are lost! And now we need to start over! I just...I can't even believe this!" She had been exasperated with research scenarios before, but she could not remember a time when she had felt so utterly disappointed and frustrated. They had been getting interesting results for the last several weeks, and she had been busily studying them and helping the others to design new experiments. It had never occurred to her that the mice could be contaminated. Wasn't that why the research facility kept their own mice in the first place, to control issues like that?

"Sarah, calm down, it's not like…"

"Calm down? What the hell are you saying, Emile? Four weeks! For four weeks we've veered from our AIDS research to work on Rhonda's latest pet project. And…there are people who have died from this virus. And the company needs to re-open the area for drilling as soon as possible. They are waiting on our lab's results! I'm supposed to meet with Angela in just a few days, for heaven's sake! What am I going to tell her? 'Sorry, we messed up. Got the wrong mice, no worries. The Arctic workers are still dying of the viral infection, but hey, we'll start over with fresh mice. Just give us another six months.' Are you kidding me?"

Emile lowered his gaze.

"Um, I think I may have something," said Kevin.

All eyes turned toward him. Sarah had not even noticed him earlier as he had been sitting quietly behind her. He had probably walked in when they were looking at the graphs. Everyone was astonished as he rarely ever said a word in any of their meetings.

Kevin swallowed audibly and made a show of putting his cell phone into his pocket before he continued. "The control mice," he said. "You asked me to look into them and so I did. It turns out that they came from two different rooms, C12 and C8."

"The mice always come from several different rooms," said Emile dismissively. "What of it?"

Kevin swallowed again. "I'm sorry, it's probably nothing, but there are different handlers in those two rooms, and I thought maybe they could have done something different to the mice..."

Sarah had a strange sense of déjà vu as she remembered her conversation with John a few nights earlier.

Emile rolled his eyes. "Kevin, it's not unusual to have different handlers. Did you speak to either of the handlers, by chance?"

"Um, no, but I thought about it. I thought maybe if they used different food or something..."

Emile gave an exasperated sigh. "Kevin, all the handlers do is feed the mice, change their water and give them clean bedding material. Nothing else. And all of the different rooms use the same supply of bedding and water and food."

"I know," said Kevin, blushing slightly and clearly embarrassed. "I just thought..." he said, his voice trailing off.

Even in her distress, Sarah realized that perhaps this was why Kevin never spoke. As soon as he said anything, all of the others jumped down his throat. "What, Kevin?" asked Sarah, trying to gain control of her voice, but Kevin did not answer.

"And, you didn't find anything else?" Emile asked, plowing over Sarah's unanswered question.

"Um, no," came Kevin's voice, barely over a whisper.

"Wait a moment," said Sarah, more in control of her temper. "Kevin might have a point." Then turning toward Kevin she asked, "Would you mind following up with the handlers? I want to know if there's anything, anything at all, no matter how insignificant it may seem, that one or the other might have done to, or with, the mice."

Kevin nodded and pulled his cell phone back out of his pocket.

"All right, so we need to figure out what those little dark purple spots are, in case they are important. Does anyone have anything else?" asked Sarah, looking around at the group.

Drew and Emile, their faces sober, did not make eye contact with her. Sarah took another deep breath. She felt as if her foot was going to snap off her leg with the pain. "So," she said, willing herself to stay focused, "what this basically means is…" Sarah let out a deep, shuddering breath. "What this basically means, is that we've lost four weeks of investigation. If our controls can't be trusted, none of our data can be trusted. Agreed?"

Sarah looked around at the glum group. No one stirred and no one met her eyes. She cursed and placed her hand over her forehead, holding her palm flat against it as if she thought her head might explode. Her head and her foot ached. She rose slowly, and with a deep frown creasing her forehead, she limped out of the lab.

In her office she sat down and placed her leg on the stool that she had commissioned for that purpose. As she sat still, she felt her pulse increasing as the enormity of what she had just been told washed over her again. It was as if she understood it, felt despair, then momentarily forgot about it and had to re-understand it. When that happened, dread would envelope her all over again.

Finally, she could bear it no longer. She ripped off her lab coat, threw it on the chair, grabbed her purse and hobbled out of the building with as much dignity as she could muster. She needed to get out and get some fresh air.

As soon as she stepped outside she was met with the wall of heat and humidity that lay over Houston in July. It had rained earlier in the day, but the scant precipitation had immediately evaporated and the entire city had become a sauna. Sarah had grown up in Reno, Nevada, where it was hot much of the year, but never this humid.

She took a halting breath, reminding herself that people in other parts of the world paid to have experiences such as this one, albeit while sitting in cramped little wooden rooms, for periods not exceeding twenty minutes and wearing only a towel. Still, after the bone chilling winters she had endured in Chicago working on her post-doc, she had vowed to never again complain about the heat.

She knew that she could not go far with her leg, so she headed in the direction of the Museum of Fine Arts Houston, which was only a couple of blocks away. As she entered the building, the soothing coolness of strong air conditioning greeted her, instantly cooling the rivulets of sweat that had begun to flow all over her body. She took the escalator down to the café and ordered a large black currant iced tea. She sat there for a long time, thinking.

The slow, though painful walk had been good for her, forcing her to concentrate on something else instead of thinking about the mice. The results just didn't make sense. They were all control mice, so why would they react in such a different manner to the same stimulus? And what were those infuriating purple dots doing on the brain tissue slides?

As she sat thinking, periodic waves of despair would wash up and roll over her. It was disheartening to lose the time. But, research in general was frustrating, she reminded herself. Sometimes years of work could be lost or wasted when things went wrong. Tropical Storm Allison, which inundated Houston with surprising ferocity in 2001, had destroyed thousands of genetically engineered mice and laboratory animals and some researchers lost their life's work. So, in comparison, this was not more than a blip.

Setbacks were inevitable. She knew that. She had *known* that and still it had caught her by surprise when it had happened to her.

She remembered a friend of hers from graduate school who had done his research in the history department, spending countless hours a day in the library, gathering material for his thesis. However, when he was done for the day or the week, he would close his books and walk away. She remembered feeling slightly envious because things didn't work that way with living organisms. One could never take the entire weekend off if a culture was growing. But, truth be told, she loved a good challenge, and there was no comparing how much more interesting it was to work with living organisms than with indecipherable writings in old books.

Living organisms. That's exactly what had gone wrong. The mice were not living. Or rather, some were thriving, and others were dying too quickly. What on earth was happening? As she sipped the last few drops of tea, now greatly watered down by the melting ice cubes, she returned to that question. There had to be a way to get to the bottom of it, and perhaps the answer would shed light on where the research needed to go afterwards. Yes. Now that she thought about it, frequently the most frustrating results led to new breakthroughs. It was probably too much to hope for right now, but even this realization went a long way toward making her feel better.

She looked at her now empty glass. The café, decorated with fake palm trees, was still fairly empty. All around her the bright blue tables were covered with crumbs and the sweat rings from glasses that had been filled with ice. Two waiters, joking in Spanish with each other, were making their way methodically down the rows of tables, disinfecting and cleaning them. As she watched, she noticed that although each worker was using the same type of cleaning spray and presumably the same kinds of cleaning cloths, the tables did not look the same when they finished wiping them. As she wondered idly about this, a new thought occurred to her.

She looked at her watch and realized that over an hour had elapsed as she had sat there, thinking. She got up and gathered herself for the walk back to the lab. She was in a better mood now that she had just thought of a new idea.

CHAPTER 15

Back in her office in the UT Medical research building, Sarah pulled up the most recent data tables and began going through them again. The idea that had begun to form while she was sitting in the café had coalesced on her walk back. If it turned out that the mice were not contaminated before the testing began, then there was one other possibility which they had not yet explored: perhaps the mice from the two groups had been handled differently while they were being inoculated with the virus. Emile had said that they had all received the same batch of virus, but perhaps some of them had squirmed more while they were being handled and had therefore ended up receiving an unintentionally lower or higher dosage?

Or perhaps some sort of contamination had occurred while they were being handled? Stress levels would have been skyrocketing among the researchers as they worked with the lethal live virus, wearing all of the protective gear and trying to be careful not to contaminate themselves. And healthy mice did move around quite a bit, even when handled correctly.

Or perhaps something else had occurred during the inoculation process, something that would tip her off as to why the mice were faring so differently. Fortunately, this was something she could attempt to verify herself as the lab kept a video feed of everything that happened in BSL-4, the lab with the highest biosafety level. This was the lab where the investigators handled the most deadly viruses, and video cameras had been installed for security, protection and training purposes.

Sarah typed in the codes to access the video feed and began the painstaking process of observing the work that had occurred in the lab over the previous weeks. Fortunately the researchers had not spent much time in the room, as once the mice were infected they had been locked in hermetic, self-contained cages, pre-equipped with plenty of water and food. After that, the mice had only been handled rarely and as needed. Sarah was able to fast forward through large stretches of the video feed, but after she had seen it in its entirety, she went back through all the footage a second time, focusing carefully on every step that the investigators had taken while they were in the high security lab.

Investigators had to be decontaminated both before entering and after exiting this lab. Her researchers all held Ph.D.'s and were drilled regularly on safety precautions. Their equipment was checked rigorously. She verified to her satisfaction that they had suited up properly, and checked the records to make sure that no flaws were later detected in their suits or gloves, and no contamination from outside had shown up on any of the control tests.

Then she watched in slow motion how the researcher, it was Drew this time, fished a mouse out from the first bin by its tail. He quickly hoisted the mouse up in his left hand and then lowered it to the surface of the table, allowing it to catch hold of a test tube rack turned on its side. The mouse immediately grasped the wire bars of the rack, which was shaped like a grid, and tried to pull itself free of its captor, who continued to hold it by its tail.

With the mouse stretched out, Drew pressed two fingers of his right hand on the mouse's back, flattening it slightly, and then, still anchoring the tail between his little finger, ring finger and the base of his thumb, he now firmly pinched the nape of its neck with the pad of his thumb and forefinger of his left hand, taking as much skin as possible in order to immobilize the torso of the mouse, pinning it down in his palm, before picking it up and flipping it over.

Thus the mouse was held in one hand, its belly exposed, its four legs sticking straight up into the air and its head unable to turn side to side to bite the hand that held it fast. That didn't stop the mice from trying to do so, however, and as Drew held the mouse, she saw its little legs kicking and its head struggling to swivel.

Soon after injecting the mouse in its belly with a quick acting muscle relaxant, the mouse stopped struggling. It was still awake—there was no need for full anesthesia—but it would not feel pain or anxiety.

Then it was time to deliver the virus. Since they wanted to be sure that the virus entered the lungs, they were using a technique called non-invasive pulmonary application. This would ensure that the virus was placed into the lower airway. Tally picked up the aerolizer, which looked like a metallic syringe. The "needle" was a slender tube which was bent at an angle so that it could be inserted into the throat of the mouse. When she pushed on the plunger, a precise dosage of solution was delivered into the mouse's trachea in the form of a fine mist. The mouse gasped for a moment, which indicated that the concoction had not been swallowed, and soon it was breathing normally again.

Once the mouse had been inoculated, it was then placed gently in a second bin. The mice would be drowsy for the rest of the day, but by the next day they would be recuperated — unless the virus was busy infecting it.

Sarah watched the procedure being repeated for each mouse, looking closely and rewinding as necessary to be sure that she had observed each step thoroughly from all of the angles of the three different cameras. When she finished, she slumped in her chair and ran her hand over her pony tail, absently teasing out the curls.

Nothing. There was nothing abnormal in the entire process. The video feeds confirmed that her researchers had been meticulous and there was no indication whatsoever that the contamination could have derived from faulty technique. Sarah sighed and turned off the video feed, now at the end of the second viewing. She rubbed her eyes. She still could not see how the results they had obtained could be explained. Why had some lived and some died across the spectrum of dosage levels? And how had some of the mice cells become contaminated with whatever those purple dots were? It made no sense. Sarah had worked with mice for years, often taking tissue samples from the brain, and she had never come across something like this before.

Her research had been devoted to finding a cure for the deadly African virus for years. Like all other viruses, HIV could not be grown on inert media, but rather required a living substrate. Most often chick cells derived from embryonic eggs were used to cultivate viruses, although human HeLa cells and even mouse cells could also be used. The cells were induced to grow on one inside wall of special rectangular shaped bottles which lay perfectly flat on trays.

A clear serum closely mimicking blood (without the red blood cells) was placed in the bottles so that the chick or human or mouse cells, growing like a translucent lawn along the bottom side of the bottle, were nourished with it. Then the cells were carefully infected with the virus which would reproduce madly, killing most of the cells. Once enough virus particles were obtained, the researchers could run different experiments on how to attack the virus.

For the initial Laptev virus experiments, her team had attempted to use both cells grown in bottles as well as live mice. However, it had soon become evident that the mice were a better option as they were mammalian cells and the virus thrived in them. Thus they had concentrated all of their efforts on using mice for the experiments.

She remained with her eyes fixed on the monitor, lost in thought. She had triple checked the techniques that her investigators had used, searching for mistakes or deviations from standard procedure that could explain the sudden change in events. None had surfaced. As the minutes elapsed, she became convinced that the contamination must not have occurred in the lab.

So, she thought, if it did not happen in BSL-4, then the mice must have been contaminated from the beginning. But how could that have happened? When did it occur? Why would only some of the mice be contaminated? And what exactly was it that had caused the contamination? What *were* those damn purple dots? Why were they only in the brain cells of some of the mice?

She looked at the clock hanging sterilely on the wall, like an impartial observer, not caring one whit about the rapidity of the passing minutes and hours which it marked. It was nearly eight. John had said that he needed to work late too, but now she called him and asked if he wouldn't mind picking her up. Her foot hurt too much to drive back to their apartment by herself.

CHAPTER 16

"You are not going to believe the day I've had, John" said Sarah as soon as she settled herself into her seat in the car. Since he had been tied up in meetings all afternoon and she had been unable to reach him by phone earlier, she had decided to just wait and tell him the whole saga in person.

"Apparently, the oil company has been putting pressure on Rhonda because they want to open up drilling in the Arctic again, so she's been coming down to my office for lots of meetings, and we have been updating her on our results pretty much on a daily basis."

John nodded, looking at her briefly and then returning his attention to the road.

"Well, yesterday morning, just after my meeting with Rhonda, Emile came to my office and told me that some of the results just didn't make any sense. I looked at his data, and sure enough. We had three groups of mice, receiving low, medium and high dosages of the virus, and they did not have the reactions that we expected."

"What kind of reactions did they have?" asked John.

"They died."

John whistled softly. "Ouch. All of them?"

Sarah looked despondently out the window at the darkening summer sky. "No, not all of them, but it still totally sucks. I mean, they didn't even do the dying part right. We had expectations about how many would be taken ill based on the quantity of virus they received, but what we got was a weird mix of mice dying at low dosages and mice living at high dosages. I just don't get it. I mean, we've been working with mice and with viruses for a long time. We're not rookies who didn't design an experiment properly. Something is definitely amiss and I haven't figured it out."

John listened quietly as he drove, but Sarah said no more. "I don't know, maybe some of the mice were different strains? Or some were hardier to begin with..."

"Good guesses, but no, they checked all that. There were a few differences between the mice, but those differences showed up pretty evenly in both groups, the ones that lived and the ones that didn't."

"*Hmm,*" said John. "Maybe the techs got the mice mixed up in the vivarium before they gave them to your lab?"

Sarah had also thought about that scenario. "It does seem like the most likely explanation, you're right, but it's baffling given the genetic similarity of all the mice. The ones that are altered with tumors or other genetic defects are usually also quite obviously different at the DNA level, and close parentage among the genetically modified ones is not common. Oh, and the other thing we found is that some of the mice seem to be...contaminated with something. It's really strange."

"Contaminated," said John solemnly, and a heavy silence flooded the car for a moment. The "c" word, as Sarah sometimes called it, was a nightmare for all researchers.

"Contaminated," she repeated, seeing the annoying purple dots in her mind's eye. "I don't know for sure, but we saw these strange little specs in their brain cells. Not all the mice have them, mind you. But...actually, the more I think about it, the more those little dots look like cysts to me. I said as much to Drew and Tally, but they think it might be something else. Still, I'm only working on a hunch. I don't know how it could have happened or how these mice could have cysts in their brains without suffering any other collateral damage. It's pretty strange."

"And you're doing tests to find out what those little dots are?" he asked, pulling the car into a parking spot. One of the great things about living in an apartment building close to the museum district was their short commute, especially at this hour of the evening. They got out and Sarah leaned on John, her leg now pulsing more painfully. "We gotta get you to the couch," he said, gently leading her toward the door of their apartment.

Once she sat down and propped up her leg, Sarah sighed. "Yeah, that's where we are. Drew and Tally left a few reactions running, just to see what we can come up with. But I'm starting to think that it's also possible that those purple dots, that infection, contamination or whatever it is, may not even be involved in the way that the mice reacted to the virus."

"A red herring?"

Sarah nodded. "It's possible. I don't think they've examined all of the mice to see which ones have dots, so we don't know which ones are contaminated, or if the contamination is equally distributed among all the mice, you know. It could be that the contamination is found in both the living and the dead tissues. And maybe we just stumbled on those purple dots by chance and they don't really mean anything."

"Hmm," said John, as he put on an apron and began composing their dinner. "Well, so back to your first situation. Why would some of the mice be living while others died? You said they had the same dosage?"

"The same dosage within different groups. So you have a group of mice, say Group A, who all get a low dose of virus delivered directly to their lungs. All should live or, if they die, then most of them should die. We have about 50% dying. Then we have Group B with a higher dose of virus. If 50% of Group A died, then you'd definitely expect a higher number of mice to die when they have more virus pumped into their lungs. But they don't. It's like 48% that die and the rest aren't sick at all.

"Then we have Group C with an even higher dose of virus. These guys breathed a lot of virus and they should *all* be dead or on the verge of dying. But again, only about 50% of the mice die. The other 50% are fine and dandy. It just doesn't make sense. The effects of the viruses should be dose dependent. The more you get, the worse off you are."

John looked at her gravely, his eyebrows scrunched together, knife poised in mid-air over the carrots as he listened intently to her explanation. "Have you tried looking at other factors? Maybe they were fed differently, or maybe one group was inadvertently exposed to a vitamin?"

Sarah closed her eyes for a moment. Now that she was finally sitting down, in her own apartment, the exhaustion that she felt washed over her again. "We checked all of that too. Nothing," she said, her voice heavy and falling to a whisper, as if the words were too heavy on her throat. She sat quietly for a few minutes, watching as John expertly chopped the rest of the vegetables, lettuce, tomato and cucumber, for the salad. Then he got out a chunk of feta cheese, carefully cut off a portion of it, and crumbled it over the lettuce.

"The only difference we have seen is that Kevin said that the two groups were housed in different rooms in the vivarium. Rooms C12 and C8. But I went and took another look at both of those rooms and they are totally identical."

John shrugged his shoulders. "Yeah, I've been down there too. All of the rooms are the same, I'm fairly certain, so that shouldn't make a difference, should it? And can you tell which mice came from which room?" asked John as he turned to stir the mushrooms which he was sautéing in some olive oil and garlic. The aroma made Sarah's stomach growl lustily.

"I don't think so, but I don't think it matters. We know that some of them came from one room, and some from the other, but I don't think we have a record of which ones came from which..." said Sarah, stopping in mid-sentence. A thought had occurred to her and she sat up straighter. "Wait a minute! Why didn't I think of that before? We *can* check to see which mice came from which room. I'm not sure if that's important, but I'll text Kevin right now and ask him to compile a report in the morning. You're brilliant, honey!"

"And I thought you married me for my body," he said, chuckling and raising his arm to show a pretend muscle bulge.

"Oh, definitely that too," she said, winking and blowing him a kiss. Then she typed out her note to Kevin. Everyone had assumed that since the mice were from the same control group, they could not be traced, but the new ear tags had codes which did allow for tracking individuals, and by plugging the barcodes into the computer, they would be able to tell which room each mouse had come from. It wasn't much, most likely just another blind alley, but it made her feel slightly better to at least have one new idea to look at tomorrow morning.

CHAPTER 17

Sarah looked at her watch impatiently. It was almost 11:00 am, and she was sitting at her desk trying to focus on a report that she was writing for Rhonda. Normally Sarah would have trudged upstairs to deliver the bad news in person, but Rhonda was away for a few days at a conference in Atlanta. It was convenient timing, thought Sarah, with a sigh of relief.

"Call me as soon as anything comes up," Rhonda had said. But Sarah had decided that the best way to present the disappointing news would be in the form of a well redacted statement. However, she wasn't making much progress. If she was honest with herself, she still held out hope that Kevin would uncover something interesting about the rooms the mice came from, or that Tally or Drew or Emile would figure out something, anything, which would help them salvage some dignity. Then she would not have to say that some of the mice from each group had died and some were perfectly fine and that they had no understanding of how or why this had happened, and that furthermore, there had been some sort of contamination which she also did not understand and had no clue as to whether it was related to the mice surviving or not surviving the Laptev virus infection.

She glanced again at her watch. Only one minute had passed since the last time she had looked, but surely there would be some answers by now. She had heard nothing all morning.

She rose, walked to her door, and looking out into the hallway she saw Kevin quickly approaching her office. Walking next to him was a young woman. She was dressed in jeans, a cotton T-shirt, and tennis shoes. Her brown hair was pulled up in a casual ponytail, from which a few wisps had escaped.

As Sarah looked at Kevin, she could tell that something was amiss. It took her a moment longer to realize that for once, he did not have his phone in his hand.

"Dr. Spallanzani," he said, increasing his pace to a jog. "I think we might have something."

Sarah felt her heart skip at the news. She motioned Kevin and the young woman, whom she now recognized as Molly Greenburg, one of the vivarium technicians, into her office and sat back down at her desk. She had hoped for answers but had not expected them to come running to her in the form of Kevin.

"Dr. Spallanzani," repeated Kevin, catching his breath. "I think I found something important."

Sarah nodded, "Go on."

"Molly here, she works in the vivarium, C12," he said, now looking at Molly, who blushed and looked down at her lap.

"Yes, we've met before. How are you, Molly?" said Sarah.

When Molly didn't reply, Kevin prodded her. "Molly, you gotta tell her what you told me."

"I'm...I'm really sorry," she said, not meeting Sarah's eyes, "I never meant to do anything wrong, I promise! It's just that poor little Opus was going to be sacrificed and nothing at all was wrong with him so I felt sorry for him," her voice croaking, as if she were about to start crying.

"*Shh*, it's okay, Molly. What are you talking about? Who's Opus?" asked Sarah, confused. It was evident that the girl was upset but Sarah couldn't make heads or tails about what she was saying.

"Opus is the mouse that I took home," said Molly, her eyes beginning to fill with tears.

Sarah's eyes widened at the admission and her heart was suddenly beating boisterously in her chest. Keeping her voice steady and even, she said, "So you took a mouse home, which I'm pretty sure is against animal handling policies, but we won't go there just yet. Please tell me that it was a healthy mouse."

Kevin looked encouragingly at Molly. After a moment Molly nodded and began to speak again.

"Yes, he was healthy. Nothing was wrong with him at all. I kept him as my pet. My kid brother loves him. And Opus seemed to be pretty happy but then I got the idea that he might be missing his friends, you know, since mice are social," said Molly, her voice lowering further as she continued with her story. "So then one day I brought him back for a visit."

Sarah gasped. "You brought him *back* to the vivarium?"

Molly nodded.

"And..." prompted Kevin.

"And then, quite by accident, I promise, he…well, he got mixed-up with another mouse and spent the night at the vivarium. Dr. Spallanzani, I'm so sorry! I didn't think it would matter, just one night, and none of the mice have any tumors or anything, so I didn't think it was a big deal."

"And when you brought him back and he got a sleep-over, did he have direct contact with all of the other mice in the room?"

Molly stared at her hands, folded in her lap. Her nose had gone quite pink and she was no longer making eye contact with anyone.

"Molly, answer Dr. S., please," said Kevin gently laying a hand on her back.

Molly was still for a few more seconds, then she nodded and said in a voice that was cracking, "Yes. Well, maybe not *all* of them. I let him visit with the ones I thought were his friends. I'm so sorry!" Suddenly the tears began to flow out of her eyes and she quickly wiped them away.

Sarah crossed her arms tightly over her chest. If Molly had taken the mouse home and then brought it back, it could have carried any number of pathogens with it back and forth. That might explain the purple dots in the brain cell slides. Or it might not. There was still no telling what those dots were.

"Tell me, Molly, when did this happen?"

"I took him home, let's see, we were in exam time…"

"I remember," said Kevin, "I had a paper to write."

"You knew that she took a mouse home from the vivarium and you didn't report it?" asked Sarah, turning to Kevin.

"I'm sorry," said Kevin, breaking eye contact and blushing.

"He didn't know, Dr. S., I promise. I didn't tell anyone," said Molly.

"I...I think I did know," said Kevin quietly.

Sarah watched as Molly turned to face Kevin. Her young eyes were wide and she looked like she was seeing a stranger.

"I saw you tuck it into your backpack in the locker room," said Kevin, meeting Molly's eyes.

Molly looked incredulous. "But, I thought...you were with Tammy and I didn't think..."

"I knew that the mouse was healthy and he was going to be destroyed, so I thought it wouldn't matter," said Kevin, looking down at his own lap. "I'm really sorry too, Dr. S.," he said.

"And did you know that she had brought it back to the vivarium for a little visit?"

Kevin swallowed and blinked. Sarah noticed his long dark eyelashes. He was a handsome kid.

"No. It never occurred to me that that could happen. I...well, I guess I should have made it clear that that would never be allowed," he said softly, looking at Molly.

Sarah sighed. She was not a parent, but she remembered being young and sometimes making decisions that she would later regret. "Well, once you start breaking rules, it's sometimes hard to know when to stop," she said.

She looked at the two of them for another moment. They had made a mistake, but it was clear that they had done it out of kindness, and she really couldn't hold that against either one of them. She remembered feeling sorry for the mice too when she had first worked with them, and, she had to admit, she had also considered rescuing one or two at some point, though she had never gone so far as to actually formulate a plan and act on it. No, this was not the time for blame.

"Tell me, when did you bring Opus back for a visit, Molly?" she said in a kinder voice.

Molly turned toward Sarah. She had stopped crying but she looked like she might begin again at any moment. "It was about five weeks ago."

Sarah nodded. "All right then. Thank you, both of you, for coming clean about all of this. Is there anything else you need to tell me?"

Molly shook her head.

"And it was just that one mouse for that one night?"

"Yes, ma'am. But I did have him visit with pretty much all of the mice," she said. "I wasn't sure which ones were more his friends and I didn't want him to miss out."

"All of the mice in all of the rooms?" asked Sarah.

Molly shook her head, glancing sidelong at Kevin. "No, just in the room I work in most of the time. Just in C12. I was afraid I might get caught if I went into any other room. Plus I didn't know if Opus even knew any of the other mice."

"And you're sure you got the right mouse back now?"

"Yes, ma'am."

Sarah nodded, digesting the news. Then she sighed and looked at Molly. "Well, I'm not sure if it is important or not, but it's good that you told us. The timing of that little social visit is certainly…intriguing. We will look into all of this a bit more. Does Kevin know how to reach you, if we have more questions?"

Molly blushed, and wiping a few stray tears from her eyes, she nodded and apologized again.

CHAPTER 18

The next morning, Sarah met with Tally, whom she noticed was wearing her dark blonde hair loose today, though she had the hair band around her wrist, ready to tie it back up at a moment's notice.

Drew joined them, carrying some printouts in his hand. "We've got the results back from the mouse tissue analysis," he said, handing her the papers. "You were right to suspect a foreigner."

Sarah nodded. Ever since she had found out about Opus's visit, she had been convinced that the purple dots were indicative of an infection, but Molly had said that her mouse at home continued to look and act healthy. She had even volunteered to bring him back, though Sarah had quickly refused her offer. Still, the fact that the mouse was healthy made for an unusual set of circumstances to be sure.

"What did you find? Bacteria? Some rogue Staph infection making cysts?" she asked as she inspected the papers. *Staphylococcus aureus,* a type of bacteria that commonly inhabited the skin surface, was usually referred to as an 'opportunist'. As long as the body's defense systems were in place, it stayed where it was, living quietly on the skin and doing no harm. However, if the skin was injured, and bacteria had a chance to enter the body, it could wreak havoc in the form of a massive, sometimes fatal infection.

As the body fought the intruder, it would typically build a wall or a cyst around the bacteria in order to isolate it from the rest of the body. For the last several years, strains of Staph had developed a resistance to antibiotics, and that made them particularly dangerous. Often they resided in hospitals, where they could attack people whose immune systems were already weak.

"No, actually, it's a different organism, but not really one I've seen before. The closest I can figure is that it is a member of the Toxoplasmosis family," said Tally.

"A eukaryote?" asked Sarah, puzzled. All living organisms are divided in two groups, Sarah had often recited to her classes: the prokaryotes and the eukaryotes. Bacteria were prokaryotes, beings so small and so simple that they didn't even have a nucleus and lacked many of the cellular organelles, the machinery which made cells work.

All non-bacterial living beings, from single-celled organisms like yeast or amebas, to worms, plants, fish and reptiles and all the way up to human cells, were eukaryotes. This was an important distinction because the medicines used to fight an infection caused by bacteria, antibiotics, could not be used on eukaryotic cell infections. Infections caused by eukaryotes, such as malaria, were much more difficult to fight as their cells were more similar to human cells. This meant that medicines that would poison them would more likely poison people as well.

If the mice possessed a eukaryotic infection then there was no hope of curing them. They would have to be sacrificed and the study would have to be begun from scratch.

"Toxoplasmosis," repeated Sarah, thinking back to her pathology classes. "I thought that it was only cats that got that?"

"Yes, well, we did a brief check of the literature, and you're right, Toxoplasmosis is often associated with cats, but it can infect many different mammals. Cats are the main host, but it has been known to also reside in mice, rats, humans, and other mammals. What we don't know is how the mice could have contracted it in the first place."

Sarah snapped her fingers as an idea suddenly occurred to her. "Molly!" she said. She jumped to her feet, meaning to run out of the lab, but was immediately and keenly aware of her ankle. She made it to the nearest table and had to lean heavily on it.

Tally and Drew were watching her with concerned looks on their faces. "Can we help you?" Tally asked.

"Kevin," she said, sitting down on the nearest lab stool. "Go get Kevin and tell him I want to see him right away."

Drew left to go fetch Kevin while Tally stayed and discussed their findings with Sarah in a bit more detail. In another minute, Drew returned with Kevin trailing him, phone in hand.

Sarah smiled and said, "Kevin, you don't by any chance know if Molly has a cat, do you?"

Kevin shook his head and began typing with both of his thumbs furiously into his phone. In a few seconds it pinged with an answer.

"She says yes, but that it would never hurt Opus."

"Opus?" asked Drew.

"What's going on? Did I miss something?" asked Tally, looking from Kevin to Sarah and then to Drew, who shrugged his shoulders at her.

"That's what she calls her mouse," said Sarah.

Drew's brow furrowed. "I'm not sure I get what…"

Another ping interrupted Drew and Kevin said, "She says her cat loves him."

Cat. Sarah pictured her pathology teacher, a tall, lean man with little round silver rimmed glasses. He was a stickler for details and he had made them memorize all of the common human pathogens and their hosts. All semester long they had been expected to be able to recite the details of every infection they had ever studied. He had drilled them mercilessly. She was only mildly surprised that now, after fifteen years, she still knew so much of the epidemiology by heart.

Toxoplasmosis gondii is carried in the intestinal tract of cats. The memory came back to her clearly now. Infected cats were only contagious for a few days of their lives. People could contract the disease from being anywhere near where a cat defecated, whether it was a litter box or an outdoor sand pit or garden. These areas remained contaminated for a up to a year afterwards. Cats contracted the disease from eating infected rodents.

"Outdoor cat?" she asked.

"Yes."

And there was something about kittens commonly spreading the disease when they caught the infection from their parents. Each cat could catch the infection only once, but cats had multiple litters of kittens and they expanded the window of possible contamination.

"Any kittens lately, by any chance?" It felt really funny to Sarah to be having this conversation through a proxy, but Kevin was taking it all in stride, as if it were the most normal thing in the world. He poked furiously at his phone, and then he looked up at Sarah, obviously surprised, and nodded.

"Two months ago. Six of them." The phone immediately chimed again. He paused for another moment and then handed the phone to Sarah.

On the small screen was a picture of two adorable, fuzzy little kittens rolling around on a piece of beige, carpeted floor, with a white mouse. Sarah smiled and handed the phone back to Kevin. Then she took a deep breath and turned to Tally. "Okay, so it looks like Toxoplasmosis you say?"

"Well, it certainly is acting like it," said Tally, still obviously baffled by the interchanges. She had peeked at the phone screen as Sarah was handing it back, but of course, she didn't have the context to understand the significance. "We've got a couple more tests still running, but we should know the answers soon, like right after lunch, I think."

"Well, at least we know what they have, and how they got it," said Sarah, feeling a measure of relief for the first time in days. "I'm not saying that it's good. It's disheartening that they are infected, but there's nothing for it. I'm just glad we got to the bottom of this mystery."

"Earth to Dr. S. Hello, we still don't have any idea what you're talking about," said Drew. Sarah quickly filled him and Tally in, noticing with a bit of satisfaction how Kevin blushed further as she told the story. She left out his part of the tale, but she knew he now felt worse since he understood the enormity of what had occurred with the contamination.

"We'll need to have all of the infected mice destroyed. Kevin, will you see that that gets done right away?" Sarah asked.

Kevin nodded.

"Good. And I'll have a meeting with Rhonda tomorrow afternoon when she gets back to give her the bad news. I was trying to put it into a report, but now I'm thinking it will be better to just sit down and tell her the sordid story with all the background. Is there a blood test for Toxoplasmosis so we can make sure we're starting with clean mice when we begin the experiments again?"

"I've got one ordered," said Drew. "They're sending it overnight, so we can begin testing right away."

As Sarah walked slowly back to her office, she realized that there was something about all of this that was still niggling at the back of her mind, but she couldn't figure out what it was. The good thing about being injured, she thought again, was that it forced her to slow down and look at things more deliberately. With each step she took, she went over the events in her mind again.

They had created the mice model controls. The procedure had been done correctly. The mice were all related genetically. Some lived and some didn't. They also knew that Molly had admitted to bringing her mouse to visit the other mice. And now some of the mice showed evidence of what might be a Toxoplasmosis infection. What was she missing?

She reached her office and sat down behind her desk. She glanced at her watch and realized it was after 1:00 pm, much later than her usual lunch time. As if on cue, her stomach grumbled. She reached for her thermos bag and fished out its contents.

As she sat munching on her apple, she once again pulled up Emile's charts of the mice and began reviewing them. Her conversation with Kevin and Molly from yesterday kept circulating in her mind, now in the forefront, now further behind, but never entirely out of sight. It seemed plausible that Molly's mouse—what had she called it? Opus? Strange name. It was likely that Opus had become infected with Toxoplasmosis when it had interacted with the kittens, and then it had shared the infection with the other mice when she brought him back to the vivarium. Mice were gregarious, Sarah thought, and Molly was probably right in that it had most likely missed its friends in the lab.

But to bring it back like that, without permission, and then get it mixed up and leave it overnight? What a tremendous blunder!

Well, there was nothing for it now. At least, she repeated to herself for the tenth time, at least they had gotten to the bottom of it. They would have to test all of the mice they had not yet used from that room in the vivarium. C12. That was the room where Molly worked. Were there enough mice from other rooms to begin the trials with the Laptev virus again soon? And meanwhile all of the mice that they had used, all of the ones still living, would need to be destroyed. They should begin with a clean slate.

Sarah scrolled through more tables and found a new one that had just been uploaded that morning by Tally. In this one the mice were tracked by their numbers, the ones on their ear tags. She was about to click to another screen when something made her stop. She looked at the table again. The mice were labeled, 'C12-229, C8-456, C12-237, C12-241, C8-514', and so on.

It was clear that the C12 and C8 prefixes came from the rooms in which the mice had been housed, while the second part of the label identified each particular mouse.

Sarah stared at the numbers in the columns and once again something niggled in the back of her mind. There was something that she was missing.

"Look carefully, Sarah," she said to herself in a low voice. What was it that she wasn't seeing? What question should she be asking that she wasn't asking? For research, she knew, wasn't just about getting data, it was about seeing patterns and figuring things out from the data in front of you.

Sarah allowed her mind to wander briefly. She remembered learning about Alexander Fleming, the man who had discovered the antibiotic, penicillin. It was in the late 1920s, and he had not been looking for it. He was doing an altogether different experiment with pathogenic bacteria, and one of his plates had become contaminated with a mold.

Contaminated. The word set off a little ripple in her thoughts.

When other scientists working with bacteria had had mold contaminations, for they were ubiquitous, they had thrown away their experiments. But instead of despairing at losing his work, Fleming had scrutinized at the contamination on his plates and observed a clear halo around the wavy, green pastille of a mold colony.

Contamination.

The fact that the halo was clear meant that there were no bacteria growing there as there otherwise should have been, for he had seeded the entire plate evenly. Then he had asked why there were no bacteria growing near the mold colony. Could it be, perhaps, that the mold was secreting an invisible toxin, something that killed life? An *anti*-biotic?

He had then isolated the clear part of the agar from the halo around the mold colony and had extracted this poison, and sure enough, it had worked against the bacteria he was testing, *Streptococcus pyogenes*, which causes strep throat. With still a further leap of imagination, faith, and genius, Dr. Fleming had taken some of that poison that was killing the bacteria, that antibiotic, which had come from a mold named *Penicillium chrysogenum*. He thus named it penicillin, and administered it to a little boy suffering from strep throat, a vicious disease that often took the lives of its victims. Would this poison also kill the bacteria inside the boy, without harming him?

Contamination. Antibiotic. Sarah looked at her computer and flipped back to the charts, scanning the graphs once again. Suddenly, one set in particular caught her attention. These graphs were plots of the number of mice still alive after they had been infected with the virus. As was expected, most mice had died from the Laptev virus, but there was a group which did not die.

Contamination.

Sarah now clicked on these individuals. On a hunch, she grabbed a pencil and a yellow pad of paper and made two columns, which she labeled ML and MBD, using Emile's joking but apt acronyms for the mice that lived and the mice that didn't. But instead of putting ticks to count numbers of mice under each heading as her researchers had done, Sarah wrote down the numbers of the individual mice. When she finished, her eyes widened in astonishment at the results and she let out a soft whistle.

She sat for another minute, letting the newfound information wash over her, and then suddenly a horrible thought struck her. She picked up her phone and scrolled through the contacts list, but could not find Kevin's number. She looked down at the moonboot still on her leg and realized she would take too long to walk down to the student area to look for him. She tried dialing the numbers for Tally, then Drew and then Emile. None of them answered. She closed her eyes and thought for a moment, then with shaky hands she dialed the student's lounge. The phone rang once, twice, three times. On the fourth ring, someone answered.

"Kevin," she said, almost breathless with excitement and relief when she heard him answer the phone, "the mice that survived the Laptev virus, have they been disposed of yet?"

"I took them straight to the Waiting Room as you asked, Dr. S., and today is the day they do it, but let's see," said Kevin, and Sarah could visualize him in her mind's eye, scrolling through his phone. She knew he had an app for just about everything, and she suspected that he must have had one for keeping track of the mice to be euthanized as well. "Okay,' he said, pausing as if still trying to find the information she sought. "They are being kept in quarantine because of the virus, so the disposal method has to be a bit different than what normally happens," said Kevin. Then there was another pause as he presumably checked another window. "They are scheduled to be put down at 2:00 this afternoon," he said. "That's in about eight minutes, give or take."

"We need those mice!" said Sarah, knowing she probably sounded a bit crazy in her desperation. "Kevin. We've got to stop them!"

Kevin was quiet for what seemed like an eternity, and then he said, "Oh, man, it looks like the app wasn't updating correctly. I think it might be too late. Hold on…"

"Kevin, it's urgent. We need to stop those mice from being killed."

Again there was another long pause during which Sarah waited impatiently. "I've just tried calling down there," he said. "No one is answering."

Sarah swore.

"All right, Dr. S.," he said, "Stay cool. I'll run down to the Waiting Room and see what I can find out."

CHAPTER 19

Sarah waited impatiently, wishing that she could at least pace her office, let alone go down to the Waiting Room and see what was going on for herself. Would Kevin reach them in time? In analyzing the graphs and making her chart on her notepad she had realized that there were several paramount questions that these mice could answer, and losing them would significantly set her team back. She looked at the clock whose hands had inched perilously close to 2:00.

Finally her phone rang.

"Kevin?" she asked, picking up the receiver quickly, "were you in time? Are the mice all right?"

"Sarah. Sarah, it's me," came the voice of her mother. "Is everything all right? You sound a little worried. Is your leg bothering you again?"

Sarah cursed silently. The land line phones in the building were supposed to have caller ID, but for some reason it only kicked in several seconds after the phone call had been initiated. She looked at the little screen and sure enough, it read SPALLANZANI. "No, Mom, my leg's fine..."

"Oh, good. Listen, I called because I wanted to talk to you about your father. You'll never believe what he did today. He was backing the car out of the driveway, not his car, but mine, you see..."

Suddenly she remembered that she had not given Kevin her cell phone number so if he dialed this number and it was busy, he might wait to call back. She had to get off the phone right away. "Mom, Mom, Mom! I'm really sorry, but I'm in the middle of something right now, can I call you back in a little bit?"

"Well, darling, I was going to tell you about your father..."

Suddenly Sarah was worried. What if something had happened and here she was, rushing her mother off the phone. Her father was in his 80s, after all, and although his health was generally robust, these things were a matter of time, she reminded herself. What if her mother had important news? "Is everything all right? Has anything happened to Dad?" she asked, her voice softer.

"Well, no, he's fine, but you see he was backing the car out of the driveway..."

Sarah's relief came and went in the blink of an eye, and now she remembered that she needed to get off the phone with alacrity. "Mom, please, I'm really sorry but I'm waiting for an urgent phone call. Let me call you back in a few minutes, once I hear from this other person." Sarah quickly put the phone down.

As she waited, her impatience rose. She was frustrated that her ankle was taking so long to heal. She was upset that the mice had been contaminated. And now she was worried that the contaminated mice, which she had thought were a burden, might turn out to hold answers, but they wouldn't be able to find the answers before the mice were killed. She rose to head toward the door, then changed her mind and sat down heavily. Her father's words to her as a child came back now. "Be patient, Sarah. Patience is a virtue. All in good time."

Then she remembered her freshman roommate saying, "Patience is a virgin," and that made her smile.

Suddenly the phone rang. Sarah hesitated, wondering if it might be her mother again. She stared at the little screen but all it said was "INCOMING CALL." Not the least bit helpful.

"Kevin?" she asked.

"Dr. S.," he said, breathing heavily as if he had run all the way to the Waiting Room. Maybe he had.

"Yes?" she asked, fearing the worst.

"Got 'em," he said confidently. "Where do you want 'em?"

Sarah said a silent prayer of gratitude. "Thank you so much, Kevin. Please have them sent to the lab and ask Tally to call me when they arrive. They need to stay in quarantine, so be careful. But I want every last one of them to have a special blood test."

CHAPTER 20

"We've got an intriguing situation," Sarah explained the next day. She was addressing all of her group, as well as Rhonda, who had returned from her trip to Atlanta, and Angela, who had insisted on being a part of the meeting. Sarah was not at all pleased about having these last two members attend her group meetings, but there was nothing she could do about it. She had briefly explained the contamination issue to Rhonda that morning, and Rhonda had insisted on calling Angela and having her attend the next meeting.

"I made a chart of which mice lived and which ones did not for each dilution level, and it turns out that the C12 prefix ones, meaning all of the mice that came from room C12, are the ones that survived..." began Sarah.

"'The boy that lived,' " said Shane in a mocking voice.

Sarah scowled at him.

Shane blushed and she wondered if he had meant to make his comment out loud. "Sorry, it was just the way you said it reminded me of Harry..." he said quietly. "Sorry, won't happen again."

Sarah took another breath and continued, "As I was saying, we know that we have a group of mice that lived, but what we don't know is *why* that is the case. At first we thought it was a bad thing that half of our groups had perished, but we were focusing on the wrong half of the groups and asking the wrong questions. What is clear now is that we can see this situation as an opportunity. The first question we need to ask ourselves is why did the C12 group live?"

Everyone was silent for a moment as they pondered Sarah's words.

"What if the mice were resistant to the virus because it has undergone a mutation and it was no longer virulent?" said Tally.

"If that were so, wouldn't more mice than just half have been resistant?" asked Miquela.

Tally nodded, "Yeah, good point."

"Well, Miquela's right that it's not likely, but it is still a possibility," admitted Sarah. "Let's try infecting a few fresh C8 mice with the same vial of virus and see what happens. Tally, do we still have that vial? Yes? Good. Would you mind taking care of that test and report back to us?"

Tally nodded, jotting down the experiment outline.

Then Sarah addressed the group again. "What else could it be?"

"What if for some reason the mice did not receive the adequate dose for infection?" asked Emile.

Sarah nodded. She was back in her element now. Ever since Kevin had managed to save the mice the day before, she had been feeling exuberant. "That's also possible, though it would be strange that only the C12 mice, which were mixed with the C8 mice, were the ones who did not receive the adequate dose. Kevin, are there any C12 mice left that we haven't used?"

Kevin jabbed his thumbs at his phone a few times. "Yes," he said, momentarily. "There are about 20 more."

"Okay, Emile, please take two of our C12 group of mice that have not been used before and inoculate them with a fresh batch of virus. Let's see what happens."

"But you don't think that either of these things are what has happened, do you?" asked Rhonda.

Sarah had to smile. "It's just a hunch," she said, "but no, I don't."

The room was silent for a few seconds.

"Well, are you going to tell us what you think might be happening?" asked Angela.

Sarah hesitated briefly while she gathered her thoughts. Her idea was a bit far-fetched and she was suddenly abashed to describe it in front of her visitors. She took a deep breath and reminded herself of the reasons why her hypothesis seemed like a good one. "Well, I could be totally in left field, but this is what I'm thinking: what if, for some reason, the mice in C12 were already resistant?"

"They can't be resistant to Laptev if they've never seen the virus and have not been inoculated beforehand," said Emile. "And Laptev is a megavirus, which means that it belongs to a group of viruses that is exceedingly rare and found only in remote locations around the planet. So it's impossible that the mice could be resistant. Maybe some of them could have had some natural immunity to viruses in general, or maybe they had some sort of interferon thing going, but it's unlikely that the whole group from C12 would be resistant, while none of the C8 ones were."

"Interferon?" asked Angela.

"It's a compound that host cells release when they are being attacked by a pathogen like a virus. It lets its neighboring cells know that there is danger around so that they can increase their defenses."

"Some call it a 'Paul Revere' molecule," said Shane. "The viruses are coming, the viruses are coming!"

"No they don't. I've never heard that," said Emile, rolling his eyes. "Anyway, Sarah, like I said, there's no way that the mice can be resistant."

Sarah looked at him enigmatically, raising one eyebrow.

"Sarah, it's not magic," said Emile, with a note of impatience creeping into his voice. "If the mice have never seen the virus, which they shouldn't have since it was locked in the ice for 30,000 years, there's no way they would have been able to create antibodies against it. We also know there are no similar viruses that infect mammals nowadays, so there's no chance of cross-immunity. There's simply no way for the mice to have developed an immune response before they were exposed."

"I agree," said Sarah hesitantly, "and we can run a couple of ELISA tests to see if the infected mice that lived have anti-Laptev antibodies."

The enzyme-linked immunosorbent assay, often called by its acronym, ELISA, was a great diagnostic tool that was often used in a microbiology laboratory as it employed antibodies, which were like precise keys, to identify certain substances. The substances thus marked would glow in the dark and could be captured in a photograph.

"Actually," said Tally, "I ran an ELISA."

"You did?" said Sarah and Emile in unison.

Tally nodded. "And it gave me an idiosyncratic answer. Look."

Sarah leaned in and watched as Tally clicked on the progressively magnified images. Her eyes widened with barely concealed delight as she watched. She had seen viruses being attacked by host defense systems many times, but she had never seen anything like this. The magnified ELISA images showed a single megavirus that was perfectly surrounded by a lustrous ring, as if the virus had donned a snug, luminous coat. The light was due to the huge antibody complexes that were attacking it. The antibodies had been labeled with fluorescent markers and she could just imagine them clustering furiously around the antigen.

When she thought of these complexes she was always reminded of Koi ponds she had seen as a little girl, which teemed with brightly colored yellow, orange and white fish. As the fish swam, their long, diaphanous fins billowed out, their tails trailing gracefully in the water. But when she threw a few pellets of food into the pond, the fish had become a writhing mass, pouncing on the pellets as if they were starving.

"I don't get it," said Angela. "What exactly are we looking at here? I see a dark elongated blob surrounded by something that shines, but I can't tell what any of it means."

"Those glowing parts you see there," said Sarah, leaning in toward the monitor and using her pen as a pointer. "Those are antibodies, thousands of miniscule immunoglobulins, each labeled with a tiny fluorescent protein. They are the mouse defense system, so they float around in the blood, watching out for any trouble. They seem to have found it so they are attaching to the foreign particle that is threatening the mouse. In this case, their enemy is the Laptev virus," she said, moving the pen to trace a large ovoid shape, the virus, at the center of a gleaming halo.

"But I can't really distinguish anything. It's all just a spiky glowing mass around the virus," answered Angela.

Drew nodded. "Antibodies are too small to be observed under the microscope. And sometimes many antibodies will link together, forming complexes." He switched to another screen which had a schematic drawing of antibodies attaching to an antigen. "The 'Y' shaped antibodies become attached to each other by the base of the 'Y', and the arms of the 'Y' stick out so as to capture the foreign particle, which is called the antigen, that they're seeking. Of course, like I just said, all of that's way too small for us to observe directly. That's why scientists came up with the idea of attaching markers, labels, to the antibodies."

"When the immunoglobulins link into a single complex, it's like putting several daggers together by their hilts and throwing them at the enemy," said Shane, and everyone turned to him. "Except each dagger has two blades instead of one. As soon as the enemy is stabbed, it becomes labeled. So it's like it has this big flag on it. So now other factors in the blood see the flag and they signal for the white blood cells, the big bad blood thugs, to come and 'beat up' the offending virus or particle by ingesting it, entombing it in a vacuole, and mercilessly exposing it to lysozyme, a noxious enzyme that breaks down and dissolves almost any viable molecule."

"That's...a good way to explain it," said Sarah, more than a bit surprised that Shane had actually contributed something worthwhile, even if his description had been rather unorthodox.

"So in these mice we can see that there are some antibodies in their blood," Tally said, "but the number is not high enough to stem a viral infection the way we see happening here in this ELISA."

"Before we go any further," said Angela, "can anyone tell me *where* scientists got a protein that glows in the dark? Did they, like, steal it from lightning bugs or something?" She smirked as if her question was outlandish.

"That's exactly what they did," said Sarah. "They cloned the genes responsible for the glowing. Now they also use genes from bioluminescent protozoa as well."

Angela's eyes widened with surprise and then, as if to cover her embarrassment, she quickly turned to Tally. "Please go on, you were saying?"

"Okay, so clearly we have the mouse's immune system attacking the virus, but that's not at all that's going on here. It's almost as if…well, no. I can't rightly say. It just seems like…"

"Like what?" asked Sarah, almost holding her breath. She was really hoping that another of the researchers would come to the same conclusion that she had.

Tally shook her head. All eyes were focused on her now, and the lab was quiet, waiting for her to finish her thought. "If I didn't know better," she said, spreading her words out as she thought, "I would say that instead of the mouse's host defense system coming to the rescue, it was an entirely different particle which was attacking the virus."

Sarah raised an eyebrow. Everyone watched mesmerized as Tally showed them some more slides in which the viral particle could be seen being engulfed by a much larger dark spot. It reminded Sarah of the first video games she had played as a child, where the Pacman, that smiley face turned profile, had swallowed those little balls.

"Whoa, what is that? It's way too big to be a part of the blood that we've never seen before," said Emile.

"I know," said Tally. "It definitely should not be there."

"But, we have seen it before," said Sarah. She waited until she had everyone's attention and then she clicked to the brain cell slides with the purple dots.

"Toxoplasmosis?" asked Drew, incredulously. "But it was in the brain cells. Now you're saying it's in the blood too?"

"I think so," said Sarah.

"I don't understand," said Rhonda. "Are you saying that the Toxoplasmosis is somehow protecting the mice?"

"I know it sounds improbable," said Sarah, "but it's what the results are showing us. Somehow the Toxoplasmosis infection is protecting the mice from Laptev HFV."

"That's crazy!" said Shane. "Why would that happen? One's a primitive virus and the other is so much more evolutionarily advanced. The two have nothing in common. How would the Toxoplasmosis even know to attack the virus?"

"I never thought I'd say this," said Tally, "but I agree with Shane."

"And I'm totally lost again," said Angela, clearly frustrated.

Sarah held her hands up in a placating manner. "I could be wrong, I admit, it's just a hypothesis, but work with me here. Toxoplasmosis was the established infection in our C12 mice, right? We don't know for sure how long these mice have been infected, but they looked healthy and acted normally when we began the experiments, right? So that means we can assume that Toxoplasmosis knows its host and the two are fairly copacetic..."

"Inasmuch as a parasite can be copacetic with the organism it is feeding on!" said Tally.

"Yes, you're right. Still, the two of them are fine, living in relative peace, when all of a sudden, in waltzes Laptev, the third wheel. Toxoplasmosis dude is not up to sharing, so he kicks Laptev in the butt. Totally gets rid of him," Sarah said.

Emile crossed his arms and gave her a skeptical look.

"You guys have heard of this happening before, right?" said Sarah, her eyes shining with excitement. "I remember studying a case like this in a Parasitology class I took a long time ago. There was a type of acacia tree whose sap was particularly appealing to a certain type of ant which crawled up and down the trunk feeding on the sap that the tree produced. The tree and the ants had a symbiotic relationship. When, however, the tree was threatened by, say, a giraffe or an antelope, which decided to feast on some of the tree's tender leaves, the ants would rush to the invader and pierce its tongue with their fiery venom, and the giraffes were soon dissuaded from making a meal of these leaves. In that manner, the ants were parasitizing an organism, the tree, which in turn they protected from another invasion by the giraffe."

Drew and Rhonda nodded but everyone else still looked doubtful.

"I think it's possible that this is a similar situation. In this case, this little Toxoplasmosis was doing the same thing that the ants did. It was protecting its host from harm by this attacking virus," said Sarah.

Angela shook her head and blew out a long breath. "Well, if that doesn't beat all."

"Do people get Toxoplasmosis infections?" asked Miquela.

"Actually, they do," said Sarah.

Everyone was silent for another moment while they digested this fact.

"Do you think, I mean, is it possible that some of the people who survived the Laptev infection in the Arctic could have had a Toxoplasmosis infection?" asked Tally.

"That's the million dollar question, isn't it?" said Sarah, now beaming.

"I'm on it right now," said Angela. "I'll have everyone who survived tested and I'll let you know the results at the next meeting."

CHAPTER 21

"Fascinating…yes, Stan, I believe this is exactly what we need. Now you can go ahead and open up drilling again," said the voice on the other end of the line.

"But, we're still not sure if that is enough of a protection," said Stan, suddenly realizing that perhaps sharing this information had been a bad idea.

"You've confirmed that everyone from the barracks that survived Laptevgate had that cat infection. That's what the blood tests revealed. And the testing at the university is showing that having the cat infection gave the mice immunity to the virus as well. Am I right?" said the voice in a reasonable manner.

"Yes, but her notes say that the data is preliminary. I was just informing you so you could be aware that progress is being made."

"And so it is, Stan, so it is. Those university scientists, and scientists in general, they always take a long time to reveal their results. They can know something for years and not come out and say it outright. They always want to do ten million more tests, and write only little parts of it up in papers, so they can get a lot of fame. I know. My father was a scientist. My brother-in-law is a scientist. They've both told me all about how those types work. But we're not that way. We're businessmen. We get things done. Now that we have the answers, it's time to open up the drilling area in Laptev Bay. Effective immediately." There was a more steely tone to the voice now, but Stan was used to it. Shareholders were not known for their interpersonal skills.

"I hear you, Dennis, but I'm still somewhat concerned. What if some of the people we send up there don't have that cat infection?"

The line was silent for enough time for Stan to become nervous. Finally he heard Dennis take a long breath through his nose.

"Tell you what. Only send people with the cat infection out to drill. Get them all those military grade gas masks. If everyone uses proper procedure when they are out on the ice, and they all detox thoroughly before they enter the camp, no one else should be affected."

Stan sighed. He was beginning to regret having informed the Chairman of the Board about the information he had found on the server in Angela's folder. Technically the folder was password protected, but as CEO, he had access to all the documents and even though she communicated frequently with him, he had continued to monitor all of her notes carefully. This operation was too important.

"I don't know. I would feel awful if we lost any more people out there. And it would be terrible PR for Riesigoil."

"For Chrissake, Stan, we've been abundantly cautious, and we hired the *best* scientists to do the research. Now we've got the data. I just don't see any need to delay any further."

Stan thought about Dennis's words. It was an arduous decision because in his heart of hearts he suspected that he was making a mistake, but his logical side could find no reasonable argument to explain his misgivings. He let out a long breath. "All right, sure," he said, "I'll give the order now."

"Oh, and Stan?"

Stan hesitated for a second. He could guess what Dennis was about to say.

"No need to share this decision with anyone, if you get what I mean. We can do this quietly. Much better that way."

"You mean Angela?"

"Yeah. Especially her. My understanding is that she still hasn't recommended that the site be re-opened, right? But, she's in Houston, and they're thousands of miles north. What she doesn't know, well, it won't hurt her now, will it?"

"When she finds out, she's going to be pissed," muttered Stan.

"Not that it matters what she thinks."

Stan said nothing.

"Why, Stan, correct me if I'm wrong here, but I would say that it almost sounds as if you're holding back on us. If I didn't know better I'd wonder...but, no, I get it," he said and chuckled lightly. "I get it. You're probably just tired. Stressful job. That's fine. Don't you worry. If she makes any problems, why then, it's a free world, isn't it? She can find herself another job, right? We've got sturdy non-disclosure agreements with all of the VP's, so that shouldn't be an issue either."

"Right," said Stan. He still felt like it was a mistake, but he also understood as well as the board did that there was an urgent need to get back on the saddle if Riesigoil was to stay competitive.

After he hung up, Stan immediately gave the authorization to open up the drilling site, and then he turned away from the screen and looked out the window. A summer storm had blown in and the rain was peeling off from the clouds in large steel colored sheets. He stared listlessly as the missile drops streaked the window panes. All he could think about was the phone conversation he had just had. Had he made a mistake in opening up the site again?

His eyes followed the heavy rain downward and he saw that the Houston streets were becoming torrential rivers. All that water, flowing swiftly and loudly to the ocean. The ocean. Suddenly he had a flashback of the Deepwater Horizon. The platform was engulfed in flames and spewing great black clouds of smoke as tiny boats sprayed large arcs of water onto it. He had watched the video multiple times, vowing that he would never forget the lives of those people who had perished in the middle of the ocean.

The truth was that he still felt guilty. As VP of Health, Safety and Environment he should have insisted that the management halt the operations until all of the safety issues had been resolved. There had been so many problems.

But each day of delay was costing the company millions of dollars, as the board had reminded him every time he broached the subject.

The storm continued to rage and Stan turned back to his desk. He felt cold. Cold. Certainly not as cold as it had been in Arctic five weeks ago when the virus had struck and all those people had perished in the barracks. Seven lives had been taken, also technically under his watch.

He turned back toward the computer screen, having decided that it had been an unfortunate decision to listen to Dennis. He never should have given the order to reopen the drilling.

Suddenly his cell phone buzzed again, startling him. It was Dennis again.

"Have you given the order to reopen up the drilling site?" he asked.

"Yes, but I'm thinking that..."

"Oh thank God," said Dennis, brusquely cutting Stan off. "We just got confirmation from our secret operative in Siberia that Glassuroil has completed their well and they are now pumping. If we don't move quickly they're going to drain the basin. And if any of the other shareholders had gotten wind of this and you still hadn't opened up the site, they would have bailed really fast. Man, am I ever glad you listened to me."

Stan hung up and ran his hand through his hair. Glassuroil was doing fine. They were up in the same area and there was nothing happening to their workers. And now Riesigoil knew what precautions to take. It would *not* be a repeat of the situation in May or of Deepwater. This was different. He was over reacting. Working too hard.

"You work too hard," his wife had complained bitterly. Incessantly. Then one day she had taken the kids and moved back to New York. Just like that.

Stan closed his eyes. He hated to remember his separation, but it must have been something about the rain that was bringing back the memory. It had also been raining fiercely on the day she had left him, nearly five years ago. Just before the Deepwater Horizon had caught fire. First his personal life had gone up in flames, followed by his professional life.

After leaving BP, he had accepted the job at Riesigoil, a company with an excellent safety track record. He had thrown himself into his work, and within two years they had promoted him to CEO.

He looked outside again and saw that the rain was finally letting up. The clouds would probably blow away within the hour and the city would become a tropical swampland, the air thick with humidity and mosquitoes.

CHAPTER 22

"You're up early," said John sleepily. "5:56. Have you been up long?"

Sarah looked up from her laptop and smiled at her husband. She loved the way he looked in the morning with his ruffled hair, so boyish. "I've been thinking about your mice that were acting braver than they should—are you still having that problem?"

John walked over and started the coffee machine. "Actually, yes," he said, drawing the word out as he fought with a yawn. He shook his head, as if to clear it. "We have narrowed it down to one small group that is not acting normal. We've got them isolated and we're not including them in the study for now until we figure out why they are so different from the rest."

"Do you think it might be related to what Molly told us about bringing her mouse back for a visit? Since we found out that our mice have Toxoplasmosis, I've been wondering if perhaps your mice might be contaminated like mine?"

John pressed his lips together. *"Hmm,* well, I guess it's a possibility. It crossed my mind briefly when you first told me about it, but I asked Trevor and he said that none of my mice came from C12."

Sarah twirled her ponytail thoughtfully and nodded. Her gaze seemed miles away. "If you want, you can send some of the little guys down to my lab and we'll draw some blood samples and run a few tests."

John held the coffee pot aloft as he stopped and reflected on Sarah's words. "Well, I guess it wouldn't hurt. What made you think of this?"

"It's something I was reading about Toxoplasmosis," she said, pointing to her glowing laptop screen. "In our meeting yesterday Miquela asked if humans can get Toxoplasmosis, so I started reading about it some more. And studies do show that Toxoplasmosis infections can affect behavior in rodents."

John grabbed a box of cereal from the pantry and reached for a bowl. "You know, now that you mention it, I actually *have* heard of those studies, but I didn't make the connection. Okay, I'll have Trevor take you some mice this morning."

"Are they infected with Toxo?" asked John as he picked up his wife's call that afternoon.

"Yes. Every last one of the mice in your group that's acting funny—not afraid of the stimuli that should frighten them—they all have it. "

John sighed heavily. "Sheeze. I was afraid you'd say that. I did some more reading on the subject this morning, and it all fits. How about the others—the ones that are acting normal?" he asked.

"All clean. Only the ones that are acting strange have the infection."

John was silent for a moment and Sarah could picture him biting his lower lip as he thought. "Well, at least that makes it easy. We'll get rid of those mice and make sure we start over with a clean batch. How do you think they caught the infection? Could it have been from when Molly worked for our side of the vivarium a few weeks ago?"

"No, I don't think it was Molly herself who carried the Toxo to your mice, but it could be that Opus, Molly's mouse, is like the Typhoid Mary of the late 1800s, early 1900s—do you remember studying about her?"

"Um, the name rings a bell, but I can't say I recall the details. Just that she got people sick or something like that?"

"You're pretty good!" said Sarah, chuckling as she spoke. "Typhoid Mary was a cook who did not wash her hands after going to the bathroom."

"Disgusting."

"Yeah, well from the number of signs in restrooms in restaurants nowadays it's something we are *still* struggling to teach people who prepare our food."

"Ugh, I hadn't thought of it that way. So Typhoid Mary got people sick?"

"Yeah, many of the people who ate her food got sick, but she, herself, didn't show any signs of infection. So she inadvertently provided the scientific community with the first example ever documented of a carrier with no symptoms—an asymptomatic carrier, as we now call them. But remember, at this time we still hadn't established the clear connection between bacteria and infections. And there were no antibiotics yet. Disease control was still partly based on superstition."

"Bad airs, evils spirits…"

"You got it! My recollection is that Mary went from house to house, in different cities, always working for families as their cook, of all things! And soon after she came to their kitchens, members of the family would get sick with typhoid. Several people even died from the disease. It took the authorities a few years to finally figure out that she was the link between all of the cases, because of course, she kept moving and didn't exactly leave forwarding addresses."

"Not surprising."

"Yeah, and to make matters worse, I think she even refused to cooperate with the doctors when they finally showed her the evidence because she didn't really believe them."

"You're kidding!" said John.

"No, her behavior was atrocious. Eventually, of course, she succumbed to the infection too, but I think they had to put her in jail to restrain her."

"Wow. Kind of makes you wonder, doesn't it? I mean, what people will say about *us* a hundred years from now when they look back at the things we're doing?"

Sarah looked down at her desk. It was a sobering topic for her. "Hopefully there will still be people a hundred years from now," she said, her voice tight. "If we keep wrecking our planet the way we are…" She did not complete her sentence. Thinking about the climate crisis and pollution always filled her with dread.

"Hey," said her husband more gently. He could always read her feelings, even over the phone. "Hey, it's going to be fine. We humans are resilient. We'll figure it out."

Sarah took a deep breath. Now was not the time to allow herself to become frightened about the future of humanity.

"Plus," said John, obviously intent on changing the subject, "we just solved this mystery, didn't we? We now know that Opus was our Typhoid Mary. And actually, it makes sense. When I got here this morning I did a thorough search of the vivarium records and I found that the group of mice that is not behaving spent some time in room C12 a few weeks ago. So, we're all good, right?"

Sarah smiled and felt a bit better. Even strong people sometimes succumbed to their fears, she knew. But her sanguine husband was right. There was still room for optimism in this world. "We're all good. Thanks, honey."

CHAPTER 23

"Wow," said Shane, "can you imagine what an effective weapon it would be?"

The entire research team, along with Rhonda and Angela, were seated in the conference room and had just begun discussing the findings from the last few days. The discovery that the mice were infected with another organism prior to commencing the study had been a tremendous disappointment, but when they later found out that this infection actually protected the mice from Laptev hemorrhagic fever virus, everyone had been surprised. Further studies had been designed and several had been completed. The results were now being reviewed.

"Weapon?" asked Tally, narrowing her eyes.

"For fighting the virus, hello! If everyone who has a Toxoplasmosis infection is protected, then that solves that problem in record time," Shane said and snapped his fingers. "All we have to do is develop a vaccine with the live infection, and presto! And, oh, here's a great idea:

what if it turned out that Toxo protected us from other major pathogens as well? Wouldn't that be amazing? This could usher in a whole new era for disease control! All of our concerns about finding new antibiotics or worrying about the toxic effects of drugs that we now use might one day be null and void. It would be a whole new world, a complete revolution in medicine."

"Whoa, hold on here a moment. You can't really be serious!" said Drew.

"Why not? Think about it: if having this infection protects you from terribly dangerous viruses and possibly other pathogens..."

Sarah's jaw tightened. "Wait. Just stop a minute here, Shane, you are definitely going too far. Do you realize the implications of doing something like that? I mean, if I understand you correctly, you're saying that we should consider infecting humans who are *not* ill with this known pathogen in case they come in contact with Laptev HFV?"

Shane hesitated. "Well, maybe not everyone, but just the ones who want to work in the Arctic."

Angela nodded and scribbled furiously.

"Hang on!" said Rhonda, joining in the fray. "What you are suggesting would be wholly unorthodox, unethical and I seriously doubt the FDA would approve anything like this without tons of clinical studies. Do I need to remind you that Toxoplasmosis is a *known* harmful pathogen? It's a teratogen. It can cause terrible birth defects in human fetuses. We couldn't possibly ask people to receive live vaccines with Toxoplasmosis and take that risk."

Sarah nodded. "Rhonda is right. Even if we were sure that an infection of Toxoplasmosis would have the exact same effect in humans as it does in mice, which, by the way, is a huge leap, it would take years of studies to be sure that it was safe. Years. Plus there's the fact that it's entirely possible that it doesn't behave the same way in humans at all."

"But don't you see? We *are* sure that it behaves the same way. Angela said that all of the survivors of Laptevgate had Toxo. Max, that bear hazer guy, he had a whopping infection. That's what the results showed," said Shane.

Angela nodded her head vigorously. "He's right."

"See? So I don't understand why everyone is so bent out of shape. There are already millions, or I should say, *billions* of humans infected with Toxoplasmosis. I was reading that it's probably somewhere between thirty and fifty percent of the population of the world that have this infection now," declared Shane, crossing his arms.

"But we still don't know if it has other effects on humans," said Drew. "What part of the body does it inhabit normally anyway? Do we even know that? Is it the same as in mice?"

"It hangs out in the brain. In both mice and humans," said Tally.

Drew bristled, his face reddening. "The brain? Are you kidding me? Oh, man, that's terrible. You're saying we should infect humans with a pathogen that we know inhabits the brain? That's insane! What if it has an effect on their behavior or their memory or something? We have far more questions than answers at this point."

Shane shrugged his shoulders. "I honestly don't see what the big deal is. Many people already infect themselves willingly. Look at cat owners."

"Oh, come on, Shane! Be reasonable here. Not all cat owners have Toxoplasmosis, not even by a long shot," said Tally.

"How do you know? Have you tested them all?" shot back Shane. Sarah could see that this was becoming heated, but she preferred not to interfere yet. There was a place for healthy debate in science, and a meeting such as this was a good one.

"Look," said Shane in a quieter voice. "I was reading an article about a researcher who has studied Toxo in humans and he claims that tons of cat owners are infected, and they don't even know it. And probably even if they did know it, they wouldn't care. All they care about is having a cute little kitty," he said, the pitch of his voice rising for the last few words. "Does anyone ever stop to consider the consequences before buying a cat and bringing it home?"

"Shane, what are you saying? There's nothing wrong with bringing home a kitty cat!" said Tally, throwing her arms up. For a second it had looked as if she was ready to slap Shane, but it was probably just Sarah's overactive imagination.

"Look, it's all of you who need to be realistic. These people, they let their cats into their homes, allow them to play with their children, walk on their kitchen tables and cabinets, sleep in their beds. It's no wonder they become infected. And, good for them. Now they are protected. So what would be the big deal in helping other people who don't have cats get protected too?"

Sarah felt the blood rising to her face. "Shane," she said through nearly clenched teeth, "what you are proposing is heretical. Didn't you hear what we just said? It's way too dangerous to even think about 'vaccinating' people with Toxo."

"Actually, I don't get it," said Angela, speaking up. "I mean, I'm certainly no expert, but it sounds like Shane is right. Haven't cats been domesticated for centuries? It's not as if cats were some exotic and unknown pet, some rare lizard or South American rodent! We're talking about house cats. They have been human pets since...well, for a long time. I mean, even the Egyptians had cats thousands of years ago."

She paused and ran her hand nervously over the surface of the table, back and forth, as if erasing some unseen blemish. "So my question is, if cats were causing this bad infection, this Toxospasmosis or whatever it's called, how come we've never heard of it before? How come we don't have all sorts of warnings and regulations about cats? Surely the fact that cats are so widespread means that the cat infection that's protecting the mice from the Laptev virus is actually not a bad thing."

Shane straightened his shoulders. It wasn't every day, Sarah thought wryly, that the VP of a large company agreed with him in public.

"See?" said Shane, turning toward Tally, his eyes shining. "You know she's right! You don't want to admit it. Cats, even though they can and do infect humans with Toxo, are no more a threat to our society than dogs or fish or any other normal pet that people keep. So why shouldn't we look seriously at Toxo as a tool for fighting diseases?"

"Actually, Shane," said Emile, clearing his voice before he continued speaking softly, "I think you are mistaken about the role of cats as carriers of the pathogen."

Shane narrowed his eyes at Emile who raised his hands as if to fend off Shane's anger. "I like cats and I've always had them as pets. But Angela," he said, turning to face her, "with all due respect, I think you're not understanding the whole history of cat domestication. When Shane told me his ideas last night I went online and did some sleuthing. Cats may have been domesticated, as you say, thousands of years ago, but it wasn't until the 1700s that people actually began bringing them *into* their homes.

"And it turns out that Drew's hunch is correct. The incidence of human behavioral alterations, many people call it mental illness, coincidentally began to skyrocket at about the time it became popular to have cats inside the home. Coincidence? I think not. We don't know for sure, but more and more evidence indicates that the increase in crazy, irrational and antisocial behavior among humans is quite possibly caused by a huge increase in undetected and untreated Toxoplasmosis infections in the population of people who own cats or have come into contact with cats. Which is pretty much everyone."

No one spoke for a moment while they thought about what Emile had just said. At one point Kevin's cell phone beeped, but he quickly silenced it.

"So, if I understand you correctly, Emile, you're saying that people got crazier the more cats were kept indoors?" asked Angela.

Emile nodded, and opened up the lid to his laptop.

"You've got to be kidding me!" said Angela, tossing her head dismissively. "I swear I've never heard anything like that in all my life!"

Emile was unperturbed by her reaction and continued to tap on the keys of his laptop, calling up the name of another file. Then, punching the "Enter" button with a flourish, he said, "Well, that's what the records are showing. Take a look. It was in the seventeen hundreds when mental illness started to become much more prevalent in our society."

"Wow," said Tally.

"Look, if you don't believe me," said Emile, turning his screen toward Angela. "Here are the articles that I bookmarked."

Everyone leaned in and Sarah could see the tabs of the various articles.

Emile began clicking on each one of them. "It's contemporary stuff. There's this investigator, lives in Czechoslovakia. Great story. He began examining himself when he found that he was exhibiting what he considered strange behavior. He wasn't afraid to jaywalk even in traffic and wasn't afraid of speaking up against the fascist regime that could imprison him for doing so. He saw that all of his friends and colleagues were afraid and so he began to wonder why he wasn't and if it could be that something was physically wrong with his brain. He had a blood sample taken and found that he had the Toxoplasmosis infection. After that he started studying brain cysts caused by Toxo and sure enough, those behaviors were typical of other men who had the infection."

"You mean other *people*, don't you?" said Angela.

"No, oddly enough, men have different reactions to the infection than women. Men who are infected become more aggressive and take more risks whereas women who are infected become more social and take fewer risks. It's pretty odd," said Emile.

Sarah passed Emile the plug to connect his computer to the projector and soon his screen was visible on the whiteboard. He clicked on the first article and Sarah began skimming through it, her mouth slightly open as she read.

"So," said Emile, "before we know more about what Toxo does, we cannot even consider it as a 'weapon.' We would need to do a lot more studies."

Shane frowned but did not say anything else. Instead he opened up his own laptop and began tapping away.

"All right, I think it's pretty clear that Emile has a good point," said Rhonda, looking at both Sarah and Angela. "But where does that leave us now? What's the next step?"

Angela was silent so Sarah said, "Well, what if we try to take a look at how Toxoplasmosis is protecting its host, the mouse, from the virus? Maybe there's a chemical or a group of compounds that it's producing, and if we can isolate them and characterize them, maybe we can reproduce them and use them to cure or protect people who might acquire Laptev HFV? Maybe if we can give them the chemical, instead of the whole infection, we could avoid having cysts in our brains to fight the virus."

CHAPTER 24

That evening as John cooked dinner and Sarah sat at the kitchen table, peeling carrots, he said, "Sarah, I need to go over some results with you. I've been reading a lot more about Toxoplasmosis infections, since we found out that the mice have it. And do you remember how we were talking about the fact that the infected mice behaved differently? Well it turns out that this happens not only in mice, but in humans as well."

"Yeah," said Sarah. "One of my researchers, Emile, do you remember him? He said the same thing in our meeting this morning--that it makes people crazier, though I'm not sure if everyone believed him."

Now that she thought about it, she remembered that Emile had said something else. He had looked up her story about the ants, the acacia tree and the giraffes. It turns out that recent research indicated that the ants were not protecting the tree after all. They were mere bystanders, stepping in, yes, but not effectively keeping the grazers away. When scientists had done an experiment in which they isolated the trees, putting fences around them so that no large animals could eat the shoots, the trees had not thrived and the ants had all disappeared. She had meant to follow up on that story, but had become distracted with something else.

"Earth to Sarah," said John. He had stopped cutting the tomatoes and was waving a hand at her.

"Oh, sorry. Tell me, how do you think that Toxo affects humans?"

"Well, I guess let's first start with mice. What I was reading is that they become more bold and daring. They are not afraid of cats and in general they are more likely to take risks. It's the kind of behavior that was puzzling me before we knew what was going on. "

"Not afraid of cats?" Sarah echoed. "That does sound crazy. That could get them killed."

John nodded.

"And you're sure it's because of the Toxoplasmosis infection? It's one thing to not react because they are paralyzed with fear as you expected, but it's quite another to not be afraid of cats."

John tested a piece of pasta, then stirred the pot some more. "We saw this in our lab, but I've since verified that labs in other parts of the world have seen the same behavior."

Having finished with the carrots, Sarah put down the peeler, crossed her arms and leaned back in her chair. "But, it doesn't make sense to me. If the mice take more risks, as a result of having a Toxoplasmosis infection, as you've seen, then fine, it must be that Toxoplasmosis is somehow contributing to having this happen. But what I don't see is how can that behavioral change be advantageous to the organism causing the change? If the host dies because it is taking more risks, then the parasitic organism won't live on either because it will no longer have a home. So it doesn't make evolutionary sense, does it?"

John shook his head, having tested the pasta again. Then he donned heavy oven mitts and carefully poured the pot of boiling water and spaghetti into a large colander placed in the sink. "I'm not sure either," he said, speaking through a cloud of vapor, "but I did read that it has another host..."

Sarah grunted and smiled, shaking her head. "Dear me! I'm forgetting all my Parasitology. My professor would have killed me. Of course, I get it. And it does make sense, now that I think about it. Do you remember ever hearing about the life cycle of *Dicrocoeleum dendriticum*?"

John returned the strained pasta to the pan and added a pat of butter, then began stirring the pasta with a fork, burying the butter so that it would melt. "Can't say that I have," he said, looking over at her with a mischievous smile, "but I bet I'm about to."

Sarah grinned. "Oh, it's a cool story. You'll enjoy it, I promise. Hand me those plates and I'll get us set up here."

John reached for the carrots, rinsed them and then placed a couple on each plate. Then he served the pasta and the sauce, and Sarah began her narrative.

"So, *Dicrocoeleum* is a protozoan, just like Toxoplasmosis. Scientists had studied it for years, but they had never been able to map out its complete lifecycle. They knew that there were three animal hosts that it required, and that it would spend only part of its lifecycle in each host."

John nodded as he ate, and Sarah reached for the parmesan cheese. Then she began swirling forkfuls of pasta onto her fork, and continued telling her story between bites. "So, this parasite, *Dicro*, would mate in one host and lay eggs, but the eggs would have to be transferred to a second host, a totally different animal, in order to develop. In this second animal host the little larvae would grow until they got to a particular stage, but after that, they couldn't develop any further until they got moved into a third animal host. Scientists had worked out two of the animal hosts, sheep and snails, but it took them years to come up with the third one. Any guesses as to what it was?"

John scratched his chin and frowned in an exaggerated manner, as if deep in thought. "I don't know, maybe a wolf or a fox?"

Sarah shook her head, taking advantage of the pause to eat more.

"Maybe a mountain lion—or some big predator that eats sheep? Humans?"

"You're cold," said Sarah. "Think smaller."

"Okay," said John, drawing out the last syllable of the word and rolling his eyes toward the ceiling. "If it's not a predator of the sheep, then maybe it's something that eats the snails? A bird or something?"

Sarah shook her head again, clearly enjoying the game. "Nope, nothing that eats the snails or the sheep."

"If it doesn't eat the sheep or snails," said John, handing Sarah another piece of garlic bread, "and the snail already eats something from the sheep, then it's gotta be something that the sheep eats. But, sheep eat grass and plants—does this *Dicro*-whatever—I already forgot its name—but does it live inside plants, maybe? Or an aphid or something like that?"

"No, but you are so close!" said Sarah, laughing. "The third host is ants. When they found out that it was ants, scientists were even more puzzled. *Dicrocoeleum* begins its lifecycle in the intestines of sheep, and it is excreted in sheep dung and left on the fields, right?"

John nodded. "Yeah, that much I got. And snails eat the sheep dung. It's kind of gross to be talking about this at dinner, you do realize that?"

"Oh, sorry," she said, blushing.

John chuckled. "It's all right, you're good. Just kidding. Go on."

"Right, okay. Well, the organism needs to reproduce inside the snails so that part was easy. But then it also needed to live in ants for part of its lifecycle."

"A rather inconvenient requirement if you ask me. So, pray tell, how does *Dicro* go from snails to ants? Do ants regularly make meals of live snails? Or maybe, I know, they eat the dead snails," he declared triumphantly.

"Awesome answer, but nope, wrong again," said Sarah.

They had both finished eating now, but they were still sitting at the table. They often lingered this way, talking for hours. It was one of the many things Sarah loved about their marriage.

"All right, Dr. Spallanzani, I almost hesitate to ask, but do tell," he said beckoning her to come sit on his lap.

She didn't know why, but nothing seemed to turn him on more than a mental challenge. "Well, Dr. Chadwick, you may not believe this, but it turns out that the species of ant that *Dicrocoeleum* likes to live in is partial to snail slime."

"Ugh! Now that is really gross."

"You're telling me!" she said, laughing, and then darted her eyes sideways, as if she was revealing highly classified information, and lowered her voice. "But did you know that snail slime is high in protein?"

"*Umm*, no, but I can just see it now in one of those health food shops. 'Would you like some snail slime to go with your alfalfa smoothie, sir?' "

Sarah burst out laughing, which made him laugh too.

"So the ants go and gather balls of slime and take them back to their ant hills. The *Dicrocoeleum*, which had been living in the snail's gut is released in the slime, so when the ants eat it, they get infected. So far so good," said Sarah, rolling her neck as he began massaging her shoulders. "But, the problem is that the last stage of this parasite requires them to return to living in sheep, and sheep don't eat ants."

"Don't they?" he asked, nibbling one of her ears.

"Pay attention," said Sarah, turning to face him.

"Okay, sorry," he said. "Ants don't eat sheep."

"John!"

"All right! Don't get upset! And sheep don't eat ants. I got it. So this *Dicro*-dude is screwed."

Sarah shook her head and crossed her arms dramatically, feigning annoyance unconvincingly.

"Well, are you going to finish your story?"

"Do you want me to?" she asked.

"Actually, what I want you to do is, *hmm*," he said, giving her a meaningful glance, "but it can wait. Please tell me now how the ants get into the sheep," he said wrapping her in an embrace.

"Well, as you probably know, sheep eat only the top of the grass or plants, which is why they are great natural 'mowers.' "

"That's true!" said John enthusiastically.

Sarah looked at him questioningly.

"I mean, I remember hearing on the radio how the city of Los Angeles had hired a shepherd and his sheep to 'mow' all the grass on the hills around the city and it was so much cheaper and better for the environment…anyway, yeah, let's finish your story."

Sarah smiled. "Okay, so sheep eat the tops of plants and ants hang out on the ground or under the ground."

John cocked an eyebrow at her.

"So, it's sheer genius of nature. The *Dicrocoeleum*, once eaten by the poor unwitting ant, chews through its intestine and enters into its nerves, traveling to its anterior ganglion—the ant brain, if you will."

"I do know what an anterior ganglion is!"

"Of course. Once it gets there, it changes the ant's natural behavior. Instead of being geotropic, you know, loving being in holes in the ground, it makes the infected ant become negatively geotropic."

John stared at her for a moment. "So, what are you saying? The ant goes and hangs out at the top of plants…"

"You got it! No self-respecting sheep is going to go around eating ants—they are strictly vegetarian."

"Of course," said John in a teasing voice, massaging her shoulders again.

"But if an ant is hanging out at the tip-top of a grass blade, it will 'accidentally' get eaten, thus completing the lifecycle."

"Whoa, now that is pretty cool,"

"Amazing and absolutely true."

John thought for another moment. "So, mice that are braver because they have the Toxoplasmosis infection…"

"…are more likely to get eaten by cats, thus completing the parasite's lifecycle," said Sarah.

"I see," he said. "Okay, that makes sense. That's what those research articles were saying."

Sarah got up and sat in a chair so that she could face him.

"But your story here leads me to wonder," he said, "if the parasite could be having an effect on human behavior as well?"

Sarah nodded. "One of the crazy suggestions that came up at the meeting was to inoculate people with Toxoplasmosis—or Toxospasmosis, as Angela calls it—to protect them from Laptev, but if it is causing behavioral changes or even mental illness, then it would be all the more reason why we *don't* want to get more people infected. Can you imagine the disaster if more people, even non-cat owners, were infected with an organism that can cause them mental illness in order to protect them from the virus?"

John nodded. "You're right. It could be a bad situation. It would make no sense to do that."

"I know, but I can't help wondering if maybe there is a way to control the cat pathogen so that it doesn't make us ill? We already know that there are tons of people with low-level infections, and the vast majority of these people are not crazy."

John looked at her skeptically.

"Well, everyone is a little crazy, infections notwithstanding, but you know what I mean," said Sarah. "Look around. Tons of people own cats. The vast majority of these people aren't a menace to society. But if there are people out there who are Laptev HFV-resistant, that could be a real advantage. I'm thinking that I would like to get blood samples from those people and test the samples against the virus. It would be great to know which ones are more resistant and why. And of course we could investigate what other effects Toxoplasmosis has on their lives. Are they living longer or shorter lives? Is it affecting their behavior in any way? Which reminds me, Emile mentioned that Toxo affects men and women differently. Do you know anything about that? "

"No, but considering that it's affecting behavior, it's not that surprising."

"He said it made the men more fearless and the women more social."

John smiled. "You're really getting into this, aren't you? I mean, more than you thought you would just about a month ago when Rhonda dropped the bomb on your lap."

Sarah looked down at the table and thought for a minute. Her husband was right. Only a few weeks earlier she had felt so betrayed that her team had had to turn on a dime and begin investigating a whole new topic, and now they were all engrossed in their new line of investigation.

"Yeah," she said. "I really am."

"And you're making a difference, too. I mean, you all have uncovered more than you thought you might. Do you think it's going to be hard to go back to HIV in just a couple of weeks?"

"Yes," she said again. "It will be hard. I guess in the back of my mind I was kind of hoping that if Riesigoil was really content with the work we're doing, and if they could continue to provide the funding, we might just keep going with it for a while. Especially now that it's become so interesting with the Toxoplasmosis variable thrown in."

John took a deep breath and reached for Sarah's hand. "But they're not in it just for the science, you know. They're an oil company."

"Many companies sponsor ongoing research projects."

"True. But we don't know if Riesigoil will."

Sarah looked down at the floor. In her heart of hearts she knew he was right.

CHAPTER 25

Shortly after she arrived at lab the next morning, Sarah was greeted by Emile. He had a frown on his face and was shaking his head.

"I just got back from the vivarium," he announced. "I had a call waiting this morning as soon as I got in. Sarah, it's about the mice that Kevin rescued from the Waiting Room the other day."

"The ones that survived Laptev because they had the Toxoplasmosis infection?"

Emile nodded. "Since bringing them back we had kept them all together in the same cage as they need to be in special quarantine since they could be contagious. Still I didn't expect this to happen," he said, shaking his head again. "They're all dead."

"What? How?" Sarah's face flushed and her throat felt tight. Maybe they had been wrong and the Toxo infection had not protected them after all?

"I'm not really sure, but it's a real mess, blood everywhere. It looks like they basically got in a huge fight and bit each other to death. In all the years I've worked with mice I've never seen anything like it."

Sarah shuddered. "Are you sure it wasn't hemorrhagic fever? I mean, with the blood and all."

"No, it's not hemorrhagic fever. These are definitely bites. They severed feet, ears and limbs. Some mice died biting each other's throats. It was gruesome and brutal."

Sarah grimaced. "My goodness! What do you think came over them?"

"I don't know. I guess we'll get tissue samples and see if we can see anything, but I doubt it. In any case, it really sets us back. I think Kevin said there were still some more C12's left and we can look at infecting them, maybe this afternoon."

Sarah thought for a moment. "Let's hold off on the inoculations till we get some results from the tissue samples. I wonder if it could be related to the mice having the Toxoplasmosis infection..."

Emile looked at her questioningly. "What makes you think that?"

"John was saying that he'd seen signs of aggression and fearlessness in his C12 mice, and I can't help but wonder if maybe having the virus somehow exacerbated that behavior. How are the other C12 mice faring?"

"I haven't looked at them yet, but they are all still being kept separate, so I expect that even if they are also feeling aggressive, they haven't had an opportunity to do anything about it."

Just then Sarah's cell phone rang. She glanced at it and saw that it was Rhonda. Perhaps the news had already reached her?

"Sarah, do you mind coming up to my office as soon as you can. I need to speak with you."

Sarah reminded Emile to be scrupulous around the dead mice, in case the virus had become even more perilous, and then headed up to her boss's office. Her leg was finally feeling a lot better, and the doctor had allowed her to stop using the boot as long as she kept her ankle wrapped. She was allowed to put more weight on it now too, on the condition she didn't over-exert herself. Sarah took the elevator up to the fifth floor, and when she entered the office, Rhonda's secretary waved her in.

Sarah sat down in one of the leather chairs that Rhonda had facing her desk. As usual, her eyes immediately strayed to the awards and accolades that inhabited the wall beside Rhonda's desk before she met her boss's eyes. She was trying to think of a way to break the bad news about the mice when Rhonda greeted her.

"Sarah, I've got some great news for you and your team: I asked you to come up here because I wanted to give you the message in person. You can go back to your HIV research effective immediately," said Rhonda, smiling a broad smile that did not reach her eyes.

Sarah's eyes widened and her mouth dropped open. Several weeks ago, this announcement would have been exactly the kind of news that she considered "great," but now it seemed almost like a punishment. She and her team were really getting some interesting results and to be pulled from the project so suddenly was not what she had expected.

"I don't understand," she said cautiously. "We were making such great progress."

"That's just it! You made excellent progress. Lived up to, no, surpassed everyone's expectations. And like I promised, it was only a short-term project. You, yourself told me how much you hated to leave your research. Well, now you can go back to it right away."

Sarah shook her head. "But, I...did we do something wrong? Was Riesigoil upset with us?"

"No, of course not. Like I said. It's all good."

"I just...I'm sorry, Rhonda. I don't buy it. Why would they rescind our contract overnight like that?"

Rhonda looked at her shrewdly. "All right, Sarah, fair enough. It is rather sudden and I will admit that I asked the same question."

"And?"

"They said no, that your work had been terrific. And they gave the university an even larger grant than they had originally promised, with the stipulation that a large chunk of it was to go to your lab. Look," she said, handing Sarah a letter.

Sarah took the letter and scanned its contents. Sure enough, her lab was mentioned, by name, and the sum figure attached was incredibly generous. Instead of the four or five years of AIDS research, she now could afford at least eight years, and she could hire three more full-time investigators. It was more than she had ever acquired from years of filling out grant applications from the National Science Foundation and other large benefactors.

Sarah smiled half-heartedly. "I, it's quite generous, you're right. It's just that it all seems...so precipitous. I would have thought that Angela..."

"Well, apparently Angela is no longer working at Riesigoil. But the man I spoke to said that they will be funding more research at other labs across the country as well, and that for now, this was all they needed from us. Oh, and they've asked us to turn over all of the lab notes and records."

"Really? Why?" Sarah felt her insides contract. Why was Angela no longer working there? And why did they have to turn over everything? What was going on?

"Well, there's confidential material there—names of workers, descriptions of Riesigoil practices in the field, things like that. We signed a document when we first received the research funds stating that we would hand over all data and notes once the research concluded."

"But, Angela?"

"I honestly don't know, Sarah," said Rhonda more gently. "Oscar was vague and this new man was brief. I'm telling you all that I know."

Sarah lowered her eyes. She didn't really want to confront Rhonda, but she was deeply disappointed with the news, so she said quietly, "I think this is a mistake."

Rhonda raised an eyebrow. "Maybe so, but we don't really have a choice, I'm afraid. So, if you'll please forward those records to me, I'll get them to the new gentleman. After that you'll need to destroy your copies."

Suddenly Sarah remembered her conversation with Emile. "Rhonda, I meant to tell you when I first got here. We've had some troubling news about the mice that were infected with Toxoplasmosis and the virus. This morning we found them all dead."

Rhonda raised an eyebrow. "*Hmm*. What do you make of that?"

"Well, I'm not really sure, but I had just asked Emile to begin some tests to see…"

"Unfortunately, I'm afraid we can't do any more tests."

"But, just to finish this part and find out what has happened. You see, Emile also found out that the original scenario that we had envisioned, with the symbiosis, is flawed. You remember how I talked about the ants protecting the acacia tree from invaders? It may not be true. So I was thinking that maybe the protective effect of Toxo is only temporary. So we ought to look into it a bit further. Surely they won't have a problem with that. And it could be really important."

Rhonda shook her head. "Sarah, I understand how difficult this is, but I have unequivocal instructions that we are to immediately cease all research and send in the notes today."

"But, what if the deaths of the mice are significant?" insisted Sarah. "What if it has to do with the Toxo infection? I mean, we don't know anything about this, but what if there's a similar reaction in humans who are infected? It could be really serious."

Rhonda looked at her skeptically. "Now we know that's not the case because such a huge portion of our society is infected with Toxo. We know it's at least 30% of humans, some studies indicate that it could be as high as 50%," she said, repeating the statistics that Emile had cited in the meeting a few days ago. "So clearly having Toxo does not make people more violent."

Sarah still felt that the new problem was too important to ignore. "But don't you think we should at least perform a few more tests to see why this happened with the mice?"

"No. I really don't think so, Sarah. Tell you what, I'll call the new man, Peter-something, this morning and let him know the results, and if he changes his mind, and wants the lab to follow up, I'll let you know. Okay? But I honestly doubt it."

Sarah nodded. There was nothing left to say. She returned to her lab feeling numb. It didn't really make sense that her work, and that of her team, could be jerked around so much like that. She felt almost violated. Sure, she and her team had not spent countless months on the work—it had really only been about a month, slightly less than Rhonda had originally promised. But they had made so many discoveries and so much progress. She really detested having to give up now.

She phoned Tally and asked her to gather everyone for a meeting and did not look forward to the hurt and disappointment she knew would emanate from each of their faces when she told them the news.

After her meeting with her researchers, Sarah walked over to John's lab. She walked slowly, using her cane occasionally. A cool front had come through the night before, and the humidity had broken, so the air was warm, bright and pleasant instead of overly humid and stiflingly hot. As she walked, Sarah looked around at the green grass and mounds of flowers growing convivially around the stone corner signs. Ahead of her, two dark brown grackles, their beady eyes shining, cawed harshly.

"Maybe you're reading too much into it," said John, once she had explained the situation.

"I don't know. I just can't help feeling betrayed, in a way. And I am still apprehensive about what happened to the mice."

"But they'll make you turn in all your notes, right?"

Sarah nodded. "Worse than that. I got a call from Rhonda right after my meeting with her, saying that Riesigoil had hired a team of 'data experts' to come in, capture all of our notes and erase the files. All at our convenience, of course, as long as it was today. She said they were doing it this way to 'save us valuable time and energy.' It's pretty obvious that they don't trust us."

"I'm surprised they aren't going to try to erase your memory too!"

Sarah chuckled. "Don't give them any ideas, John!" she said and gave him a hug. "They have already reminded us of the non-disclosure agreements we signed when we began the research."

"So, back to HIV now?" he asked.

Sarah nodded. "Yeah, I don't know. I'm not in the mood to go back to it like I was before. But I guess that with time we'll all get back into it. At least there are no companies waiting to stop that research. And you'll continue looking at the Toxo effects on your mice behavior?"

John smiled. "Of course! And we'll probably need your expert advice from time to time."

"All right," she said, her shoulders hunched as if the weight of the morning were a heavy burden she was trying to bear. "Thanks for the pep talk. I'd better head back over."

As she walked slowly back, Sarah once again replayed the events of the last few weeks in her mind. They had been assigned a nearly impossible task of trying to learn something about a hitherto unknown supersized virus. They had made loads of progress in figuring out its mode of transmission and had come up with a plausible theory about its history in the region. They had also found another infection which seemed to provide a measure of protection against it, and then had been summarily told to stop all work.

It didn't seem fair. Perhaps Rhonda was trying to make her life difficult so that she would resign? Well, that wasn't going to happen. She thought back to her work with HIV, and suddenly she remembered Emile's words about the relative insignificance of Laptev-HFV when compared to the havoc wreaked by AIDS. *If it were destroying small villages in some remote third world country, we wouldn't even be looking at taking on this project. And no one would be asking us to drop AIDS research, when HIV affects so many thousands of people, just to take on this tiny outbreak in the Arctic.*

He was right. Their research on AIDS *was* consequential. She would return to it proudly and inspire her team to do the same. The difference would be that now they had more money at their disposal, they could work for a longer period of time and she could be more directly involved. It wasn't such a bad thing after all, she thought, and with a lighter heart, she returned to the IDI.

EPILOGUE

Stan Sundback was checking his e-mails, even though it was almost 2:00 am and he really should have been asleep by now. It was a nervous, reflexive habit. Ever since he had authorized the re-opening of the drilling sites in the Arctic, he had been extra attentive, always half-fearing the worst.

It hadn't helped that Angela had resigned as soon as she found out about the site being re-opened without her approval. That had been another scandal, losing her. She had been strident as she accused him of being "irreverent with the lives of others" by agreeing to open up the drilling areas without further tests. Her words had stung him all the more since they mirrored his own doubts, but, he reminded himself, the job of a CEO was not supposed to be a bed of roses.

Three weeks had passed and everything seemed to be perfectly fine. It was true that they had taken extra precautions and only people who were Laptev HFV resistant had been allowed to work on the drilling sites.

Finding Laptev resistant workers had turned out to be quite easy in the end: a simple blood test showed whether anyone had the little "cat critters" as he called them—that infection that came from owning cats and somehow provided immunity to Laptev. He didn't understand the science, but then again, he didn't need to. His job, as the shareholders frequently reminded him, was to make sure that the company made money. Ever since Angela had learned from the researchers at the university that there was a way to ensure that the workers would be protected, things had gone smoothly for Riesigoil. With any luck they would have an active well started before the weather turned colder in September.

Stan yawned and placed his cell phone on his bedside table, then went to the bathroom to brush his teeth. He was concerned, to be quite honest, because Dennis had told him today that Glassuroil had just closed down its Arctic drilling stations because there had been "incidents" as of late. The intelligence reports had not mentioned what the nature of these "incidents" was, but he was attempting to convince himself that they were due to the thawing conditions in the Arctic. Maybe the melting permafrost had made it difficult to sustain the scaffolding above the well? Certainly the melting permafrost had caused havoc as the unpaved roads were now disappearing at an alarming rate. Stan had seen that this was a problem in many areas inside the Arctic circle, especially places like Alaska where the hard, frozen roads had served for decades.

Surely the incidents at Glassuroil had nothing to do with any viral outbreaks. Nothing at all. That kind of thing could not have been kept secret.

After wiping his face and hands with a towel, Stan returned to his bed and picked up the phone to silence it before turning in for the night. That's when he saw that there had suddenly been a frantic list of emails. Isolated words, 'urgent', 'six dead,' 'compound not responding,' flashed across the message subject lines.

Holy shit, he thought, and his heart began pounding fiercely in his chest. His fingers were shaking so hard that he fumbled a few times as he scrolled through and read the most recent one. It was from a minute ago, 2:09 am.

We cannot reach anyone at the compound to confirm the report that was received a few minutes ago.

Suddenly his phone rang. He saw that it was the new VP of Health, Safety and Environment, Peter Shoemaker, and immediately took the call.

"Stan, sorry to wake you."

"I was up."

"I just got a call from Riesig-Alaska, the control facility that is working with the Laptev Bay barracks in the Arctic. It seems there's been a shooting. They got word that one of the workers, I guess it was the bear hazer, Max something, who had just returned from one of the drilling sites this evening. Apparently he went crazy and began shooting. They said several people were dead. Someone from the barracks sent hasty messages and then all contact with them was lost."

"God…" Stan said, closing his eyes. A shooting. Workers dead. It was his worst nightmare. He swallowed twice before he was sure that his voice would not tremble as he spoke. "What do you suggest?"

"Since no one is responding, it could be a hostage situation. I think we need to get a plane to go there immediately and see what's happening," said Pete.

THE LAPTEV VIRUS   231

Stan let out his breath. "Okay, do it," he said, hoping against hope that it would not be too late.

Oscillating between fear, guilt and anxiety, Stan was not able to sleep for the rest of that long night. With tattered nerves he rose before dawn, fervently wishing he could turn back the ruthless passage of time and remove all traces of his permission to open the drilling site anew. He had left his phone on, but no new information had been forthcoming. He shaved, showered and just as he was walking out the door, another call came in, this time from Riesig-Alaska. He stepped back inside his house and took the call.

"Mr. Sundback," said the voice, "this is Gerald Jemison, from the Alaska Riesigoil outpost. Dr. Shoemaker said we were to call you directly as soon as we had information about the compound at Laptev Bay."

"Yes, what did you find?"

"Sir…I regret to inform you that at this time there appear to be no survivors."

Stan reached for the wall as the room tipped slightly. "What else have you got?" he said, his voice suddenly hoarse.

"We're sending photos of the bodies to our forensics team, and the authorities have been called, of course. It's too early to speculate, but what we can confirm is that most of the crew was killed in their sleep. They were shot in the neck with bear tranquilizer darts. It looks like a few of the people must have woken up while the systematic killing was going on, and there is evidence of a struggle afterwards…though, like I said, no one seems to have survived. We will keep you informed as soon as we find out more."

Stan hung up. His mind was reeling and his heart was leaden. He knew the next step that he needed to take and he mentally prepared himself to call Dennis. He tried to pick up the phone but suddenly felt nauseous. He ran to the bathroom and bent over the toilet as his stomach heaved repeatedly.

Regret and remorse took turns washing over him anew in huge, towering, suffocating waves. The image of the Deepwater Horizon, listing to the side with huge black plumes of smoke, flashed in his mind. Eleven Dead, Sixteen Injured. Then he saw the reports about the incident in early May and the headlines that read 'Seven Dead in the Worst Accident Ever in Riesigoil History.'

He covered his mouth, trying to prevent further retching, and walked to the sink to splash some cold water on his face. As he held the towel, the images which had burned themselves onto the fabric of his tortured mind continued to flash mercilessly.

He had *known* that it was a bad idea to open up the Arctic for drilling again. There were some places too remote and too wild to be dominated by humans. His own arrogance as the CEO of a powerful company had kept him from understanding this basic fact. Now the blood of all those people was on his hands.

He closed his eyes. He knew with utter certainty that there was no way he could make the call and listen to the heartless board again. There was no way that he could ever report to work again. There was no way that he could ever look in the mirror at himself without hating the monster he had become.

He carefully walked back to his bed, his head still throbbing, and retrieved his cell phone. He scrolled through the gruesome photos that Peter had forwarded to him just a few minutes ago. After he had seen them all, he gingerly turned the phone off and placed it on his night stand. Then he hesitated before slowly reaching down and opening the drawer. There it was, shiny, black and always ready to protect him in case of an intruder. With trembling hands he reached in and removed it. He held it for a moment, feeling the weight of the cold metal in his palm. He thought again about the deaths of all those people in the Arctic. He had personally met with each worker on the team before they had returned to work and he had assured them that they would be safe. It had all been a lie.

He looked at the cold, black barrel, but in his mind's eye, he saw the workers. Strong, healthy people who would never return home to their loved ones. He had watched them kiss their spouses and children before they boarded the plane.

He was so ashamed. There was no other way. He opened his mouth and the last thing he felt was the icy steel, as bitter and cruel as a stormy night near Laptev Bay, against his teeth.

THE END

ACKNOWLEDGEMENTS

My humble thanks go first to the researchers, professors and scientists who formed and inspired me throughout my academic career, beginning with the professors of Microbiology at Miami University, Oxford, Ohio. I also thank my professors at the Universidad de León, León, Spain, where I did my Ph. D., and my fellow graduate students, many of whom I still count as close friends now, almost thirty years since we first met.

I would also like to thank Dr. Chantal Abergel and Dr. Jean-Michel Claverie, whose fascinating work with giant viruses was one of the inspirations for this novel. I am deeply indebted to these two researchers and their team at the IGS, CNRS-AMU, France, for kindly providing the picture used on the cover of this novel. It's not every day that one is brave enough to write to the world's leading expert on a subject, introduce one's self, and then make a request for a photograph of their work. It is even far less often that the person receiving said request actually bothers to answer one so graciously. I am humbled and much appreciate their kindness in attending to my request.

In a similar manner, Mr. Graham Blackbourn, Director of Blackbourn Geoconsulting, was most generous in allowing me to download the image of an oil rig in the Laptev Sea area from his website for use on the back cover of this novel. His kindness is most appreciated.

My writing coach and editor, Lauren Sapala, deserves my most fervent appreciation for encouraging me in this endeavor as soon as she found out that I was on this journey. In spite of a heavy schedule and an imminent personal deadline, she made time for me. Her extensive comments on my work, both along the way and once I finished, were extremely positive and helpful, and the story benefitted enormously from her keen insights.

Special thanks go to my fellow grad student and dear friend, Dr. Carmen Guerrero, for critical reading of the manuscript, especially regarding every part of the story concerning the mice. She also provided me with the story of how researchers try to make life easier on the lab mice.

Thanks also to Theresa Kleintank, with her eagle eye for spotting typos that everyone else missed. If there are any left, it's my fault entirely for messing with the manuscript after she last saw it!

As always, many thanks to Daniel for his help with the cover of this novel and his enthusiastic feedback about the plot. I also appreciated Tania's comments and the encouragement from Pedro and Adriano who were excited about this book and reminded me regularly of this.

My loving and supportive husband deserves buckets of applause for his multiple readings of the manuscript and careful attention to all parts of the story, especially the scientific studies, to make them as credible as possible. He was my sounding board, my cheerleader, my brainstorm buddy and my best friend throughout this process.

The Laptev Virus began as a personal dare, on the first day of the 2014 NaNoMo, (National Novel Writing Month, which is always in November.) I was inspired to take this dare by the many bloggers and writers who have done likewise in previous years and posted their compelling tales, so thanks to all of you too, whoever you are.

AUTHOR'S NOTES

Most good stories have strong roots in truth, and that is also the case with THE LAPTEV VIRUS. I first got the idea for writing this novel from an article I read about the discovery of Megaviridae, and Giant viruses which were orders of magnitude larger than any that had ever been seen before. Drs. Jean-Michel Claverie and Chantal Abergel, working at the Structural & Genomic Information laboratory (IGS, CNRS and Aix-Marseille University) are world renowned experts in this area, and it was one of their latest discoveries, the *Pithovirus sibericum*, found under the permafrost and believed to be 30,000 years old, which became the premise for this novel. The researchers stated clearly that this Pithovirus is not a human pathogen, but they suggested that there could be others which are pathogens and are lying dormant in the frozen soil.

Their original scientific publication, (Legendre M, Bartoli J, Shmakova L, Jeudy S, Labadie K, Adrait A, Lescot M, Poirot O, Bertaux L, Bruley C, Couté Y, Rivkina E, Abergel C, Claverie JM (2014) *Thirty-thousand-year-old distant relative of giant icosahedral DNA viruses with a pandoravirus morphology.* Proc Natl Acad Sci U S A. 111: 4274-4279) can be found on-line and should definitely be read by all who are interested in the fascinating topic of these colossal viruses.

While I'm on the subject, I would like to take a moment to congratulate Drs. Claverie and Abergel and their team of researchers on their discovery of the still viable 30,000 year old *Pithovirus sibericum* which has been cited as number 53 in the **Top 100 Stories of 2014** in the scientific journal, *Discover*.

The Los Angeles Times story that I use in the Prologue of this novel is an excerpt of the actual article that appeared on that date, but there were some factual errors in the report which, with the help of Dr. Claverie, I have corrected. Those corrections are in brackets.

Obviously, the *Houston Chronicle* article that is read in Sarah's lab is entirely fictional.

Good stories also have parts that are exaggerated for effect, and I willingly admit that I took liberties with several truths. First and foremost, of course, is the fact that *none* of the giant viruses (which I call megaviruses in the novel, though technically the viruses discovered in the Arctic do not belong to that scientific genre) discovered to date in different parts of the planet are human pathogens. I cannot help but agree with Dr. Claverie and his team that finding pathogens we thought were eradicated, or of which we were not aware, is one of many perils that comes with the melting of our polar ice caps. It may just be a matter of time before we find a cousin of smallpox or some other nefarious pathogen which had been frozen in time.

Another area where I stretched the truth was in the speed with which Sarah and her colleagues made discoveries. If only research could progress so nicely and so quickly! I think most of humankind's problems would have been solved by now if research could naturally occur at the pace it does in this novel. But, alas, as all of my colleagues in science will quickly vouchsafe, research is arduous and there are far more dead-ends than discoveries.

The stories I tell about Fleming's discovery of penicillin, Typhoid Mary, using an electric blanket on the mice to help them wake up from anesthesia better, the part about mice reacting differently to male and female handlers, the story of Koko the gorilla, the intriguing discovery of the lifecycle of *Dicrocoeleum*, the discoveries of the Czechoslovakian scientist who has a Toxo infection himself, and the ants, acacia and giraffe symbiosis, including the modification to this last story in later years, are all true to the best of my knowledge. And

Graeter's really is, hands down, the best ice cream I've ever tasted.

Toxoplasmosis, however, is strictly a pathogen and has never, ever been implicated in protecting someone from another infection. It is a teratogen, which means that it can cause serious birth defects to fetuses. It is transmitted through contact with cat feces, and really can linger in soil for up to a year or more. This is another reason to avoid gardening without gloves.

Also, there really are high numbers of people with undetected Toxoplasmosis infections across the world, and it has been implicated in mental illness, especially as of late. There are some really interesting articles on the web about the subject. I have put the links on my website: www.christyesmahan.com

As a way of acknowledging the contributions that so many scientists have made over time, almost every one of my characters has a last name of a scientist. I encourage my readers to look up the last names and learn about these scientific contributions, especially those Redi and Spallanzani.

Finally, although I have a disclaimer at the beginning of the novel saying that all of the characters and events depicted are from my imagination or are used fictitiously, I think it bears repeating, especially since I pick on BP. Stan's experience is entirely fictional and I could have very easily chosen a different oil company as his former employer as there have been so many unfortunate accidents. It is the nature of the business and as long as humanity continues to demand fossil fuels, we will have issues with drilling and refining accidents.

If you have any questions or comments for me I hope that you will seek me out on Facebook, Goodreads or my blog and let me know!

Thank you for reading this novel. I would very much appreciate it if you would rate it on Amazon and tell your friends and families about it. If your book club decides to read THE LAPTEV VIRUS and would like to ask me questions, I would be happy to be available by Skype.